GLOBE EDUCATION SHAKESPEARE

MACBETH

William Shakespeare

DYNAMIC LEARNING

HODDER EDUCATION
AN HACHETTE UK COMPANY

Shakespeare and the Globe

Shakespeare was born in 1564, in Stratford, a small town in the Midlands. We know he was still in Stratford as an eighteen-year old, when he got married. By 1592, he had moved to London, become an actor, and become a playwright. Shakespeare died in Stratford in 1616. He probably retired three or four years earlier, having bought land, and the biggest house in the town.

Shakespeare was successful. He became a shareholder in his acting company, and a shareholder in the Globe – the new theatre they built in 1599. His company was the best in the land, and the new king, James I, made them his company in 1603. They were known as the King's Men. Men, because women were not allowed to act on the stage. Boys or men played all the women's parts. Shakespeare wrote at least 40 plays, of which only 38 survive. Only eighteen of his plays were printed in his lifetime. *Macbeth* was not one of them. It only survives because, after his death, his colleagues published a collection of his plays, known as the *First Folio*.

London Theatres

There were professional companies of actors working in London from the middle of the sixteenth century. They usually performed in inns, and the city council often tried to ban them. The solution was to have their own purpose-built theatre, just outside the area the council controlled. The first, simply called *The Theatre*, opened in 1576.

Shakespeare's Globe today

Sam Wanamaker, an American actor and director, founded the Shakespeare's Globe Trust in 1970. Sam could not understand why there wasn't a proper memorial to the world's greatest playwright in the city where he had lived and worked. He started fundraising to build a new Globe Theatre. Sadly, Sam died before the theatre opened in 1997.

The new Globe is the third. The first burnt down in 1613 during a performance of Shakespeare's Henry VIII. The King's Men rebuilt it on the same site, and it re-opened in 1614. This second one was closed in 1642, and pulled down in 1647 to build houses.

The new Globe is 200 yards from the original site, and is based on all the evidence that survives. It has been built using the same materials as the original, and using the same building techniques.

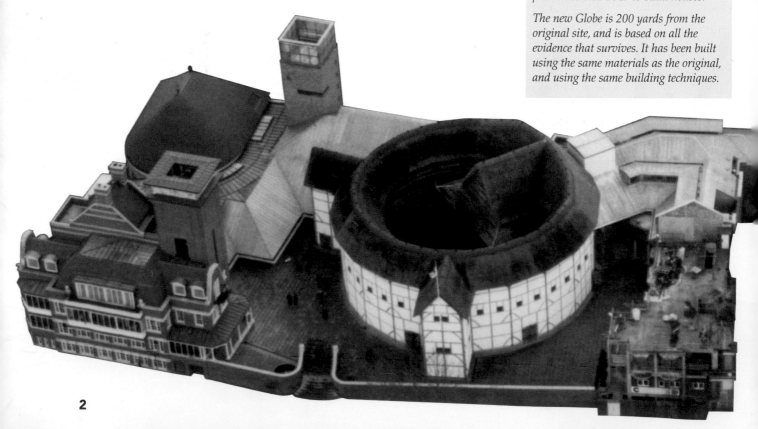

The first Globe Theatre

The Globe Theatre was open-air. If it rained, some of the audience got wet. There was no special lighting; so the plays were performed in the afternoon, in daylight. This meant that, unlike most modern theatres, the actors could see the audience, as well as the audience see the actors (and each other). It may have held as many as 3,000 people, with, perhaps, 1,000 standing in the yard. They paid one old penny (there were 240 in £1). The rest sat in the three galleries, so they were under cover if it rained. They paid more, at least two pence, and as much as six pence for the best seats. The audience was a mixture of social classes, with the poorer people standing.

The stage was large, and extended into the middle of the yard, so there were people on three sides. We think it had three entrances in the back wall – a door on either side, and a larger one in the middle. There was a roof so the actors, and their expensive costumes, would always be in the dry. The underside of this roof, called *the heavens*, was painted with the signs of the zodiac. There was also an upper stage, which was sometimes used in plays, sometimes used by the musicians, and also had the most expensive seats in the theatre. All the rest of the audience could see people who sat in the upper stage area. If you sat there, people could see who you were, that you could afford to sit there, and your expensive clothes.

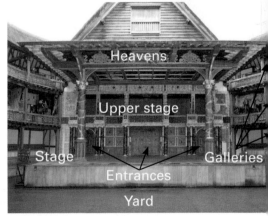

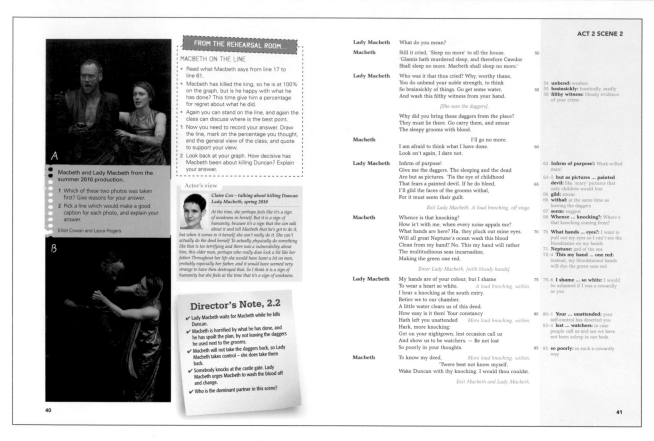

The **play text** is the place to start. What characters say is in black, and stage directions are in blue. Line numbers, on the right, help you refer to an exact place.

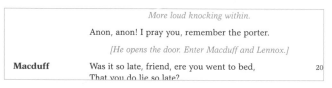

> *More loud knocking within.*
>
> Anon, anon! I pray you, remember the porter.
>
> *[He opens the door. Enter Macduff and Lennox.]*
>
> **Macduff**   Was it so late, friend, ere you went to bed,   20
> That you do lie so late?

Some stage directions, like the second one above, have square brackets. This means they are not in the original text, but have been added to help you when you read. They tell you what you would see on the stage.

> **64–5 but as pictures ... painted devil:** like 'scary' pictures that only children would fear

The **glossary** is right next to the text. To help you find the word or phrase you want, each entry has the line number in blue, then the word or phrase in black, and finally the explanation in blue again. To keep it clear, sometimes, as in this case, some words from the original have been missed out, and replaced with three dots.

Actor's view boxes are exactly what they say. Actors who have played the part at the Globe tell you what they thought about their character and some of the choices they made.

Green boxes go with the photos. They tell you what you are looking at, and give you a question to think about. Unless the question says otherwise, the answer will be in the play text on the opposite page. The names of the actors are in smaller print.

From the rehearsal room gives you the exercises actors use during rehearsals to help them understand the play. They come with questions that help you reflect on what you can learn from the exercise.

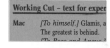

Working Cuts sometimes go with the *From the rehearsal room* activities. They cut lines from the scene so you can do the activity in the time you have available.

Shakespeare's World boxes give you important context for the play. For example, what most people at the time believed about witches is different from what most people believe today. If you understand the difference, it helps you to understand how the characters react to the Witches in the play.

Finally, **Director's Notes** boxes come at the end of every scene. They give you a quick summary of the most important things in the scene, and a focus to think about.

The Characters in the play

This book uses photographs from three productions of *Macbeth* at Shakespeare's Globe. The actors and creative teams of each production are an important part of the book.

	2001 *Director:* *Tim Carroll*	spring 2010 *Director:* *Bill Buckhurst*	summer 2010 *Director:* *Lucy Bailey*
Duncan, king of Scotland	Terry McGinty	Andrew Whipp	James Clyde
Malcolm, his son	Chu Omambala	Philip Cumbus	James McArdle
Donalbain, his son	Mark Springer	Shane Zaza	Craig Vye
Macbeth, a general	Jasper Britton	James Garnon	Elliot Cowan
Lady Macbeth	Eve Best	Claire Cox	Laura Rogers
Banquo, a general	Patrick Brennan	Matt Costain	Christian Bradley
Fleance, his son	Mark Springer	Rachel Winters	Josh Swinney James Beesley
Macduff, a nobleman	Liam Brennan	Nicholas Khan	Keith Dunphy
Lady Macduff	Hilary Tones	Karen Bryson	Simone Kirby
Son of the Macduffs		Liam Brennan	Austin Moulton Charlie George
Lennox, a nobleman	Richard Attlee	Rachel Winters	Nick Court
Ross, a nobleman	Jonathan Oliver		Julius D'Silva
Menteith, a nobleman			Michael Camp
Angus, a nobleman	Jan Knightley		Ian Pirie
Caithness, a nobleman			
Siward, an English soldier		Andrew Whipp	Ken Shorter
Young Siward, his son		Shane Zaza	Craig Vye
English Doctor			
Scottish Doctor	Terry McGinty		Ian Pirie
Captain, a soldier	Colin Hurley	Russell Layton	Michael Camp
Porter	Paul Chahidi	Russell Layton	Frank Scantori
Old Man			Ken Shorter
First Witch	Liza Hayden	Karen Bryson	Janet Fullerlove
Second Witch	Paul Chahidi	Rachel Winters	Karen Anderson
Third Witch	Colin Hurley	Shane Zaza	Simone Kirby
Hecate			
Seyton	Paul Chahidi	Matt Costain	James Clyde
First Murderer	Jan Knightley	Nicholas Khan	Michael Camp
Second Murderer	Richard Attlee	Philip Cumbus	Craig Vye
Third Murderer		Andrew Whipp	
Gentlewoman	Hilary Tones		Janet Fullerlove
	Lords, Gentlemen, Soldiers, Attendants, Messengers		
Designer	Laura Hopkins	Isla Shaw	Katrina Lindsay
Composer	Claire van Kampen	Olly Fox	Orlando Gough
Choreographer	Siân Williams	Siân Williams	Javier de Frutos
Fight Director		Alison de Burgh	Philip D'Orleans
Musical Director	Claire van Kampen	Genevieve Williams	Belinda Sykes

The three Witches from the spring 2010 production.

This production played mainly to schools. What do the Witches' costumes suggest?

l–r, Shane Zaza, Karen Bryson, Rachel Winters

FROM THE REHEARSAL ROOM...

THE WITCHES

- In small groups read Scene 1.
1 At the theatre you don't see the characters' names, you hear what they say and see what they look like. At the end of this scene, will an audience know the characters are three Witches? If so, how?
2 What else does Shakespeare tell us about what is happening in the world of the play?

ACT 1 SCENE 1

Thunder and lightning. Enter three Witches.

First Witch	When shall we three meet again?
	In thunder, lightning, or in rain?
Second Witch	When the hurly-burly's done,
	When the battle's lost and won.
Third Witch	That will be ere the set of sun.
First Witch	Where the place?
Second Witch	Upon the heath.
Third Witch	There to meet with Macbeth.
First Witch	I come, Graymalkin!
Second Witch	Paddock calls.
Third Witch	Anon.
All	Fair is foul, and foul is fair:
	Hover through the fog and filthy air.

Exit all three.

ACT 1 SCENE 2

Noise of battle offstage, including drums and trumpets. Enter King Duncan, Malcolm, Donalbain, Lennox, with attendants, meeting a bleeding captain.

Duncan	What bloody man is that? He can report,
	As seemeth by his plight, of the revolt
	The newest state.
Malcolm	This is the sergeant,
	Who like a good and hardy soldier fought
	'Gainst my captivity. — Hail, brave friend!
	Say to the king the knowledge of the broil
	As thou didst leave it.
Captain	Doubtful it stood,
	As two spent swimmers, that do cling together
	And choke their art. The merciless Macdonald
	(Worthy to be a rebel, for to that
	The multiplying villainies of nature
	Do swarm upon him) from the Western Isles
	Of kerns and gallowglasses is supplied.
	And Fortune, on his damnèd quarrel smiling,
	Showed like a rebel's whore. But all's too weak,
	For brave Macbeth (well he deserves that name)
	Disdaining Fortune, with his brandished steel
	Which smoked with bloody execution,
	Like Valour's minion, carved out his passage
	Till he faced the slave:
	Which ne'er shook hands, nor bade farewell to him,

5

10

5

10

15

20

Director's Note, 1.1

✔ The play starts in noise and mystery.
✔ The Witches plan to meet Macbeth.

3 **hurly-burly:** fighting
5 **ere:** before
6 **heath:** flat, open, windswept countryside
8–9 **Greymalkin/Paddock:** two of the Witches' three 'familiars' – their link to the world of magic, disguised as animals. Greymalkin is a cat, Paddock a toad. They are calling the Witches away
10 **Anon:** I'll be there straight away

1–3 **He can ... newest state:** He's come from the battlefield so can tell us what's happened
4 **hardy:** brave
5 **'Gainst my captivity:** to stop me being captured
6 **broil:** battle
7 **Doubtful it stood:** the outcome of the battle was uncertain
8 **spent:** exhausted
9 **choke their art:** stop each other from swimming
11–12 **The multiplying villainies ... upon him):** he has so many bad qualities
13 **kerns:** lightly armed foot soldiers
13 **gallowglasses:** soldiers armed with axes
14–5 **And Fortune ... rebel's whore:** And Fortune (the goddess of luck) sided with Macdonald, giving the rebels luck the way a prostitute gives her body
15 **all's too weak:** Fortune and the troops were not strong enough
17 **Disdaining:** disregarding
17 **brandished steel:** drawn sword
18 **smoked with bloody execution:** steamed with newly-shed blood
19 **Valour:** bravery
19 **minion:** favourite, chosen person
19 **carved out his passage:** hacked his way through to Macdonald
20 **slave:** used to show contempt for Macdonald

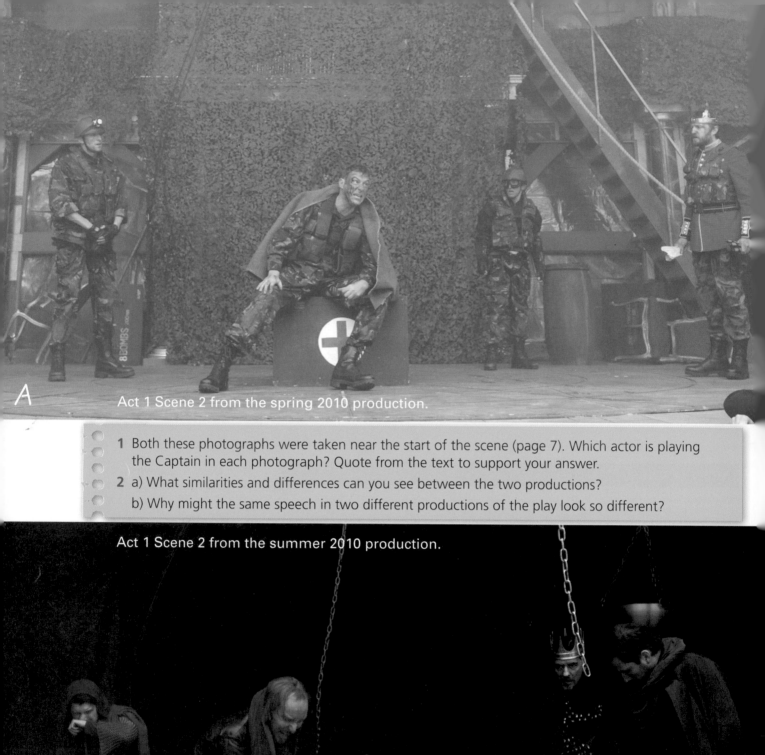

Act 1 Scene 2 from the spring 2010 production.

1 Both these photographs were taken near the start of the scene (page 7). Which actor is playing the Captain in each photograph? Quote from the text to support your answer.

2 a) What similarities and differences can you see between the two productions?

   b) Why might the same speech in two different productions of the play look so different?

Act 1 Scene 2 from the summer 2010 production.

	Till he unseamed him from the nave to the chops,	**22 unseamed him ... to the chops:** slashed him open from his navel to his jaw
	And fixed his head upon our battlements.	
Duncan	O valiant cousin, worthy gentleman!	**24 cousin:** Macbeth is related to Duncan
Captain	As whence the sun 'gins his reflection,	25 **25-8 As whence ... Discomfort swells:** Just as the sun can be replaced by storms, so seeming help can be replaced by trouble
	Shipwrecking storms and direful thunders,	
	So from that spring, whence comfort seemed to come,	
	Discomfort swells. Mark, King of Scotland, mark.	
	No sooner justice had, with valour armed,	
	Compelled these skipping kerns to trust their heels,	30 **30 to trust their heels:** to run away
	But the Norweyan lord, surveying vantage,	**31 Norweyan lord:** Sweno, King of Norway
	With furbished arms and new supplies of men,	**31 surveying vantage:** seeing his chance
	Began a fresh assault.	**32 furbished arms:** freshly cleaned weapons
Duncan	Dismayed not this	
	Our captains, Macbeth and Banquo?	
Captain	Yes,	
	As sparrows, eagles; or the hare the lion.	35
	If I say sooth, I must report they were	**36 say sooth:** speak the truth
	As cannons overcharged with double cracks,	**37 over-charged with double cracks:** overloaded with two charges of gunpowder
	So they doubly redoubled strokes upon the foe.	
	Except they meant to bathe in reeking wounds,	**39 Except:** whether
	Or memorize another Golgotha,	40 **39 reeking:** steaming
	I cannot tell.	**40 memorise another Golgotha:** make the battle as long-remembered as the 'the place of skulls', where Jesus was crucified
	But I am faint, my gashes cry for help.	
Duncan	So well thy words become thee as thy wounds;	**44 They smack of honour:** They show you are honourable
	They smack of honour both. Go get him surgeons.	

Exit Captain, helped by an attendant.
Enter Ross and Angus

	Who comes here?	45
Malcolm	The worthy Thane of Ross.	**46-7 What a haste ... things strange:** He looks like someone in a hurry to give important news
Lennox	What a haste looks through his eyes! So should he look	
	That seems to speak things strange.	
Ross	God save the king.	
Duncan	Whence cam'st thou, worthy thane?	
Ross	From Fife, great king,	**49 Whence:** from where
	Where the Norweyan banners flout the sky,	50 **50-1 flout the sky ... our people cold:** fly insultingly and fill our people with fear
	And fan our people cold.	
	Norway himself, with terrible numbers,	
	Assisted by that most disloyal traitor,	
	The Thane of Cawdor, began a dismal conflict	**54 dismal:** ominous (as if Sweno would win)
	Till that Bellona's bridegroom, lapped in proof,	55 **55 Bellona's bridegroom ... proof:** Macbeth, in strong armour, like the bridegroom of Bellona (goddess of war)
	Confronted him with self-comparisons,	
	Point against point, rebellious arm 'gainst arm,	**56 self-comparisons:** equal skill and courage
	Curbing his lavish spirit. And to conclude,	**58 Curbing:** controlling
	The victory fell on us.	**58 lavish:** wild
Duncan	Great happiness.	
Ross	That now, Sweno, the Norways' king,	60 **61 Craves composition:** asks to make peace
	Craves composition.	

9

SHAKESPEARE'S WORLD

Witches

King James I, ruler of England when *Macbeth* was written, believed wholeheartedly in witches. He was convinced that witches plotted to stop his wedding to Anne of Denmark. He had people arrested and tried for witchcraft. King James wrote a book about witches' powers, including their ability to create storms. It explained how to tell the difference between natural storms and those made by witches. It was one of many books written at the time about the powers of witches. People also wrote books challenging these ideas. However, many ordinary people shared King James' beliefs, particularly in rural communities. Witches were blamed for bad harvests, bad weather and disease (among humans and animals).

Witches were popular on the stage early in James's reign, and *Macbeth* is one of many plays they appear in. Shakespeare's witches speak in a stylised way Shakespeare sometimes uses to show a character has magical powers. Called *rhyming trochaic tetrameter*, each line has four pairs of a long syllable followed by a short one.

Director's Note, 1.2

- ✔ First a wounded soldier, and then Ross, tells King Duncan that Macbeth and Banquo have won the battle.
- ✔ Ross also tells Duncan that the Thane of Cawdor was a traitor helping the rebels.
- ✔ Duncan orders Cawdor's execution, and names Macbeth the new Thane of Cawdor.
- ✔ Duncan sends Ross to tell Macbeth.

Actor's view

Rachel Winters
Third Witch, spring 2010

With the couplets, specifically, there's a real sense of togetherness. The Witches are one. They're doing the same thing, they've all got the same goal, they are doing it together. The rhythm of the language is so different from the rest of the language in the play, which really separates them from the other characters.

The Witches, from the summer 2010 production.

This photo was taken during the first 30 lines of Scene 3. Which line do you think was being spoken? Quote from the text to support your answer.

l–r Simone Kirby, Janet Fullerlove, Karen Anderson

	Nor would we deign him burial of his men	
	Till he disbursèd, at Saint Colme's Inch,	
	Ten thousand dollars to our general use.	
Duncan	No more that Thane of Cawdor shall deceive	65
	Our bosom interest. Go pronounce his present death,	
	And with his former title greet Macbeth.	
Ross	I'll see it done.	
Duncan	What he hath lost, noble Macbeth has won.	

Exit all.

ACT 1 SCENE 3

Thunder. Enter the three Witches

First Witch	Where hast thou been, sister?	
Second Witch	Killing swine.	
Third Witch	Sister, where thou?	
First Witch	A sailor's wife had chestnuts in her lap,	
	And munched, and munched, and munched.	5
	'Give me,' quoth I.	
	'Aroint thee, witch,' the rump-fed runnion cries.	
	Her husband's to Aleppo gone, master o' the Tiger.	
	But in a sieve I'll thither sail,	
	And, like a rat without a tail,	10
	I'll do, I'll do, and I'll do.	
Second Witch	I'll give thee a wind.	
First Witch	Th' art kind.	
Third Witch	And I another.	
First Witch	I myself have all the other.	15
	And the very ports they blow,	
	All the quarters that they know	
	I' the shipman's card.	
	I'll drain him dry as hay.	
	Sleep shall neither night nor day	20
	Hang upon his pent-house lid.	
	He shall live a man forbid.	
	Weary sev'n-nights nine times nine	
	Shall he dwindle, peak, and pine.	
	Though his bark cannot be lost,	25
	Yet it shall be tempest-tossed.	
	Look what I have.	
Second Witch	Show me, show me.	
First Witch	Here I have a pilot's thumb,	
	Wrecked, as homeward he did come.	30

Drums offstage.

Third Witch	A drum, a drum!	
	Macbeth doth come.	

62 deign: allow
63 disbursèd: paid
63 Saint Colme's Inch: Incholm Island
64 dollars: silver coins
66 bosom interest: most important concerns
66 present: immediate

2 swine: pigs

6 quoth: said
7 Aroint thee: go away
7 rump-fed runnion: fat, greedy woman
8 master: captain
9 thither sail: sail there
10 like: disguised as
11 I'll do: I'll work magic on him; also suggests she'll have sex with him

15 have all the other: control the other winds
16 ports they blow: wind blowing from a port stops a ship landing, so the Witch can use the winds to keep the ship at sea
17-8 quarters that ... shipman's card: compass points on a sailor's navigation chart
19 drain him dry: exhaust him; possibly sexually
21 pent-house lid: eyelid
22 forbid: cursed
24 dwindle, peak, and pine: waste away, starve
25 bark: ship

29 pilot: person who guides a ship into a harbour

Macbeth, Banquo and the Third Witch, summer 2010 production.

The third Witch is speaking. Which of her lines do you think she is saying? Give reasons for your answer (including a quotation).

l–r Elliot Cowan, Christian Bradley, Karen Anderson

FROM THE REHEARSAL ROOM...

WALK OF FAME

- Select your favourite word or phrase that is used to describe the character of Macbeth.
- Think of a physical action or gesture that fits with your word or phrase.
- As a whole group stand in two straight lines with an aisle of about a metre wide. Make sure everybody is standing opposite somebody else.
- At the same time, everybody should call out their word/phrase with their action.
- Repeat calling out your word/phrase with the action over and over again.
- Each person takes it in turn to walk down the aisle in character as Macbeth as everybody continues to repeat their word/phrases with their action.
- As you walk down the aisle, you listen to the word/phrases and think about how it feels to walk down the 'Walk of Fame'.
- When you have finished walking down the aisle, re-join the end of the line and continue calling out your word/phrase.
- Remember to direct your word or phrase at the people walking down the 'Walk of Fame'.

1 How did it feel to walk down the 'Walk of Fame'?
2 How do you think Macbeth may have felt when he returned from the battle? Explain your answer.

All Witches	The weird sisters, hand in hand,
	Posters of the sea and land,
	Thus do go, about, about, 35
	Thrice to thine, and thrice to mine,
	And thrice again, to make up nine.
	Peace, the charm's wound up.

Enter Macbeth and Banquo.

Macbeth	So foul and fair a day I have not seen.
Banquo	How far is't called to Forres? – What are these 40
	So withered and so wild in their attire,
	That look not like th' inhabitants o' th' earth,
	And yet are on't? – Live you, or are you aught
	That man may question? You seem to understand me,
	By each at once her choppy finger laying 45
	Upon her skinny lips. You should be women,
	And yet your beards forbid me to interpret
	That you are so.
Macbeth	Speak, if you can. What are you?
First Witch	All hail Macbeth, hail to thee Thane of Glamis!
Second Witch	All hail Macbeth, hail to thee Thane of Cawdor! 50
Third Witch	All hail Macbeth, that shalt be king hereafter!
Banquo	Good sir, why do you start, and seem to fear
	Things that do sound so fair? – I' th' name of truth,
	Are ye fantastical, or that indeed
	Which outwardly ye show? My noble partner 55
	You greet with present grace and great prediction
	Of noble having and of royal hope,
	That he seems rapt withal. To me you speak not.
	If you can look into the seeds of time,
	And say which grain will grow, and which will not, 60
	Speak then to me, who neither beg nor fear
	Your favours nor your hate.
First Witch	Hail!
Second Witch	Hail!
Third Witch	Hail! 65
First Witch	Lesser than Macbeth, and greater.
Second Witch	Not so happy, yet much happier.
Third Witch	Thou shalt get kings, though thou be none.
	So all hail Macbeth and Banquo!
First Witch	Banquo and Macbeth, all hail! 70
Macbeth	Stay, you imperfect speakers, tell me more.
	By Sinel's death I know I am Thane of Glamis,
	But how of Cawdor? The Thane of Cawdor lives,
	A prosperous gentleman. And to be king

33 **weird sisters:** the Witches
34 **Posters:** fast travellers
36 **thrice:** three times
38 **Peace, the charm's wound up:** hush, be still, the spell's ready
38 **foul and fair:** refers to the bad weather (foul) and the victory (fair); it echoes the Witches in Act 1 Scene 1

40 **is't called:** is it supposed to be

43 **aught:** anything

45 **choppy:** chapped – with dry, cracked skin
46 **should be:** appear to be

51 **hereafter:** in the future
52 **start:** jump, look shocked

54 **fantastical:** imaginary

56 **present grace:** the honour he has (Thane of Glamis)
57 **Of noble having and of royal hope:** the honour he will get (Thane of Cawdor) and becoming king in the future
58 **rapt withal:** amazed by it all, in a trance

68 **get:** be the father of

71 **imperfect:** unclear, ambiguous
72 **Sinel:** Macbeth's father

FROM THE REHEARSAL ROOM...

WHERE IS MACBETH ON THE LINE?

- In line 108 the Witches' prophecies begin to come true.
- In this activity you have to decide **at this point in the play** how likely it is that Macbeth will kill the king to make another prophesy come true.
- Read to the end of this scene. At the end of the scene, how likely is it that Macbeth will kill the king?
- You can only base your answer on the things Macbeth says.
- Imagine there is a line drawn through your classroom. One end of the line represents 'he is 100% likely to kill the king'. The other end represents 'he is 0% likely to kill the king'. Think of this line as having a scale, like a graph, from 0% to 100%.
- All of the class stand at the place on the line which corresponds with your view of how likely Macbeth is to kill the king at this point in the play.
- As a class discuss why you are each standing where you are. You may need to argue your point and support it with quotations from the text.

1 Now you need to record your answer. Draw the line, mark your position and percentage, and the position and percentage that represents the majority view of the class.

2 Quote lines from the text to support your view.

14

	Stands not within the prospect of belief,	75
	No more than to be Cawdor. Say from whence	
	You owe this strange intelligence, or why	
	Upon this blasted heath you stop our way	
	With such prophetic greeting?	
	Speak, I charge you. *The Witches vanish.*	80
Banquo	The earth hath bubbles, as the water has,	
	And these are of them. Whither are they vanished?	
Macbeth	Into the air: and what seemed corporal,	
	Melted, as breath into the wind.	
	Would they had stayed.	85
Banquo	Were such things here, as we do speak about?	
	Or have we eaten on the insane root	
	That takes the reason prisoner?	
Macbeth	Your children shall be kings.	
Banquo	You shall be king.	
Macbeth	And Thane of Cawdor too. Went it not so?	90
Banquo	To th' selfsame tune and words. — Who's here?	

Enter Ross and Angus.

Ross	The king hath happily received, Macbeth,	
	The news of thy success. And when he reads	
	Thy personal venture in the rebels' fight,	
	His wonders and his praises do contend	95
	Which should be thine, or his. Silenced with that,	
	In viewing o'er the rest o' th' self-same day,	
	He finds thee in the stout Norweyan ranks,	
	Nothing afeard of what thyself didst make.	
	Strange images of death, as thick as hail	100
	Came post with post, and every one did bear	
	Thy praises in his kingdom's great defence,	
	And poured them down before him.	
Angus	We are sent	
	To give thee from our royal master thanks,	
	Only to herald thee into his sight,	105
	Not pay thee.	
Ross	And for an earnest of a greater honour,	
	He bade me, from him, call thee Thane of Cawdor:	
	In which addition, hail most worthy thane,	
	For it is thine.	
Banquo	What, can the devil speak true?	110
Macbeth	The Thane of Cawdor lives. Why do you dress me	
	In borrowed robes?	
Angus	Who was the Thane lives yet,	
	But under heavy judgement bears that life	
	Which he deserves to lose.	
	Whether he was combined with those of Norway,	115

75-6 Stands not ... belief, No more: is no more likely
77 intelligence: information
78 blasted: barren, nothing growing there
80 charge: order

83 corporal: solid, flesh and blood

85 Would: I wish

87-8 eaten on the insane root ... prisoner?: eaten the root of the plant that sends you mad?

94 personal venture: the risks you took and what you achieved
95-6 His wonders ... Silenced with that: torn between expressing his amazement and singing your praises, he's struck dumb
98 stout: brave
99 Nothing afeard ... didst make: not in the least afraid of the slaughter all around
101 Came post with post: were brought by messenger after messenger

105-6 herald thee into ... pay thee: to take you to him so he, not we, can reward you
107 for an earnest: as a token of honour to come
109 addition: extra title

113 Who was: He who was
113 heavy judgement: sentence of death
115 combined: allied to, working with

15

Macbeth with other members of the cast on stage, 2001. He is saying, *Two truths are told, / As happy prologues to the swelling act* (lines 131–2).

Which other lines on the page opposite would fit with this gesture? Explain your answer.

Jasper Britton

SHAKESPEARE'S WORLD

Asides

Asides are common in Shakespeare's plays. When a character speaks, and some or all of the other characters on stage can't hear, it is an aside. In this scene, Macbeth speaks to Banquo in a way that means Ross and Angus can't hear. He also speaks directly to audience, and no other character can hear. This is an important part of Shakespeare's craft as a playwright. When Macbeth speaks like this, he shares his thoughts with the audience. Usually, when this happens, the actor is alone on stage, and we call it a soliloquy. Shakespeare uses asides and soliloquies to show us what the character is really thinking. In the original Globe Theatre, as in today's, nobody in the audience was very far from the stage, and asides and soliloquies were very intimate.

Working Cut – text for experiment

Mac	*[To himself.]* Glamis, and Thane of Cawdor: The greatest is behind. *[To Ross and Angus.]* Thanks for your pains. *[To Banquo.]* Do you not hope your children shall be kings?
Ban	*[To Macbeth.]* That, trusted home, Might yet enkindle you unto the crown.
Mac	*[To himself.]* Two truths are told, As happy prologues to the swelling act. *[To the others.]* I thank you, gentlemen. *[To himself.]* This supernatural soliciting Cannot be ill; cannot be good.
Ban	*[To Ross & Angus.]* Look how our partner's rapt.
Mac	*[To himself.]* If chance will have me king, Why, chance may crown me, Without my stir.

Or did line the rebel with hidden help
And vantage; or that with both he laboured
In his country's wreck, I know not.
But treasons capital, confessed and proved,
Have overthrown him.

Macbeth   *[Aside.]*   Glamis, and Thane of Cawdor: 120
The greatest is behind.   *[To Ross and Angus.]*
                              Thanks for your pains.
[To Banquo.]
Do you not hope your children shall be kings,
When those that gave the Thane of Cawdor to me
Promised no less to them?

Banquo   That, trusted home,
Might yet enkindle you unto the crown,   125
Besides the Thane of Cawdor. But 'tis strange:
And oftentimes, to win us to our harm,
The instruments of darkness tell us truths,
Win us with honest trifles, to betray's
In deepest consequence.   130
[To Ross and Angus.]   Cousins, a word, I pray you.

Macbeth   *[Aside.]*   Two truths are told,
As happy prologues to the swelling act
Of the imperial theme.
[To the others.]   I thank you, gentlemen.
[Aside.]   This supernatural soliciting
Cannot be ill; cannot be good.   135
If ill, why hath it given me earnest of success
Commencing in a truth? I am Thane of Cawdor.
If good, why do I yield to that suggestion
Whose horrid image doth unfix my hair,
And make my seated heart knock at my ribs   140
Against the use of nature? Present fears
Are less than horrible imaginings.
My thought, whose murder yet is but fantastical,
Shakes so my single state of man,
That function is smothered in surmise,   145
And nothing is, but what is not.

Banquo   *[To Ross and Angus.]*   Look, how our partner's rapt.

Macbeth   *[Aside.]*   If chance will have me king,
Why, chance may crown me,
Without my stir.   150

Banquo   *[To Ross and Angus.]*   New honours come upon him,
Like our strange garments, cleave not to their mould
But with the aid of use.

Macbeth   *[Aside.]*   Come what come may,
Time and the hour runs through the roughest day.

Banquo   Worthy Macbeth, we stay upon your leisure.   155

Macbeth   Give me your favour.
My dull brain was wrought with things forgotten.

---

116 **line:** strengthen
117 **vantage:** advantages
118 **In his country's wreck:** to ruin his country
119 **treasons capital:** crimes against the state punishable by death

121 **behind:** to come

124-6 **trusted home ... the crown, Besides:** if you believe that, you might be tempted to think you'll be king as well
127-9 **to win us to our harm ... deepest consequence:** to tempt us into danger the servants of the Devil tell us trivial truths which, when they come true, make us believe their lies about more important matters (see *Shakespeare's World* box on page 112).
132 **happy prologues:** lucky opening (as to a play)
133 **imperial theme:** becoming king
134 **soliciting:** tempting, pressing a person to do something

136 **earnest:** token of honour to come

139 **unfix my hair:** make my hair stand on end
140 **seated:** fixed, held in place

143 **yet is but fantastical:** is just an idea
144-5 **Shakes so ... smothered in surmise:** So disturbs my mind that I'm constantly thinking of it

150 **Without my stir:** without me having to do anything
152-3 **Like our strange ... aid of use:** like new clothes that only fit properly when we have worn them in
153-4 **Come what ... the roughest day:** Whatever happens time will pass, and even the worst day ends
155 **we stay upon your leisure:** we're waiting for you
156 **Give me your favour:** forgive me
157 **wrought with things forgotten:** tied up in thinking of what has happened

17

Director's Note, 1.3

✔ The Witches greet Macbeth and Banquo with prophecies.

✔ Macbeth will become Thane of Glamis, and Cawdor, and then king.

✔ Banquo will be the father of a line of kings.

✔ Two nobles come from the king, calling Macbeth Thane of Glamis and Cawdor.

✔ Macbeth is distracted by the thought he might be king.

✔ How quickly does Macbeth begin thinking he may plot to become king?

FROM THE REHEARSAL ROOM...

POSITIVE AND NEGATIVE

- Split the group into three: *readers*, *positives* and *negatives*.

- *Readers* take one part each – Duncan, Malcolm, or Macbeth. *Positives* listen for, and repeat, any positive words or phrases the *readers* say. *Negatives* listen for, and repeat, any negative words or phrases the *readers* say.

- Read the scene. *Positives* and *negatives* need to listen very closely, and to repeat the words as soon as they are spoken.

1 Which positive words or phrases are spoken and who says them?

2 Which negative words or phrases are spoken and who says them?

3 What imagery do these phrases conjure up in your mind?

4 What do the words or phrases tell us about the characters?

5 How has the character of Macbeth changed from the beginning of Act 1 Scene 3? Why has he changed? Quote from the text to support your answer.

Kind gentlemen, your pains are registered
Where every day I turn the leaf to read them.
Let us toward the king. *[To Banquo.]*   160
Think upon what hath chanced, and at more time,
The interim having weighed it, let us speak
Our free hearts each to other.

Banquo   Very gladly.

Macbeth   Till then, enough.—
Come, friends.   165

                                                        Exit all.

*A trumpet fanfare is played offstage. Enter Duncan,
Malcolm, Donalbain, Lennox, and Attendants.*

Duncan   Is execution done on Cawdor? Are not
Those in commission yet returned?

Malcolm   My liege,
They are not yet come back. But I have spoke
With one that saw him die: who did report,
That very frankly he confessed his treasons,   5
Implored your highness' pardon, and set forth
A deep repentance. Nothing in his life
Became him like the leaving it. He died
As one that had been studied in his death,
To throw away the dearest thing he owed   10
As 'twere a careless trifle.

Duncan   There's no art
To find the mind's construction in the face.
He was a gentleman on whom I built
An absolute trust.

                    [Enter Macbeth, Banquo, Ross and Angus.]

                    O worthiest cousin,
The sin of my ingratitude even now   15
Was heavy on me. Thou art so far before,
That swiftest wing of recompense is slow
To overtake thee. Would thou hadst less deserved,
That the proportion both of thanks and payment
Might have been mine. Only I have left to say,   20
More is thy due than more than all can pay.

Macbeth   The service and the loyalty I owe,
In doing it, pays itself. Your highness' part
Is to receive our duties. And our duties
Are to your throne and state, children and servants;   25
Which do but what they should, by doing everything
Safe toward your love and honour.

Duncan   Welcome hither.
I have begun to plant thee, and will labour
To make thee full of growing. — Noble Banquo,

158-9 pains are registered ... to read them: I will remember daily the help you have given me

162 interim having weighed it: having had time to think about it

2 Those in commission: those sent to order the execution of Cawdor

8 Became: suited his status
9-11 been studied ... a careless trifle: has carefully chosen to throw away his life as if it was something unimportant
11-2 There's no art ... in the face: You can't work out what a person thinks and feels by just looking at them

15 The sin of my ingratitude: the fact I've not shown you my gratitude yet
16-8 Thou art so far ... overtake thee: You've done so much that it is impossible to repay you quickly enough
18 Would: if only
19-20 the proportion ... have been mine: so I could thank and repay you enough
21 More is thy due: You have earned more
24 duties: what a subject owes to a king
26-7 Which do but ... love and honour: It is our duty to do all we can to keep you safe and earn your love

19

MACBETH ON THE LINE

- This is a repeat of the activity on page 14. Look back to remind yourself of the instructions.
- Read what Macbeth says immediately before his exit (lines 44–53).
- How likely is Macbeth to kill the king at this point? Again, you need to turn this decision into a percentage and to support it with quotations.
- Again, (all the class) stand at the place on the line which fits with your view, and again discuss why you are standing where you are.

1 Now you need to record your answer. Draw the line, mark on your percentage, and that of the majority of the class.

2 What lines from the text can you quote to support your view?

Duncan, Ross and Malcolm in the summer 2010 production.

Duncan is speaking. Which line fits best as the one he says at this moment? Give reasons for your answer.

l–r James Clyde, Julius D'Silva, James McArdle

Director's Note, 1.4

- ✔ Duncan greets Macbeth and Banquo after the battle.
- ✔ Duncan announces his successor will be his son, Malcolm.
- ✔ Macbeth sees Malcolm is an obstacle to becoming king himself.
- ✔ Duncan announces he will visit Macbeth's castle, and Macbeth goes ahead to prepare. Has Macbeth decided what he is preparing for, a visit or a murder?

SHAKESPEARE'S WORLD

Succession

For Shakespeare's audience, succession – how one king or queen followed the last one – was an important political issue. From about 1590, people worried about who would succeed Queen Elizabeth. She had no children. The law was complicated, and Elizabeth refused to allow any discussion about it, so nobody was sure. When she finally died in 1603, James, already King of Scotland, was declared the next king of England.

When he became King, James chose Shakespeare and his fellow actors as his royal company – the King's Men. Perhaps this influenced Shakespeare when, about three years later, he wrote a play about Scotland and succession.

In the world of the play, though, succession is different. Duncan can choose who will be the next king. When he chooses Malcolm, Duncan makes it impossible for Macbeth to become king lawfully.

PUNCTUATION

Nominate as many people to do this activity as there is space for in your classroom.

- Read the letter aloud and start to walk around the classroom at the same time (lines 1–12).
- Each time you get to a punctuation mark, you must change direction and carry on walking.
- Continue to do this until the end of the letter.

1 How did the readers feel changing direction each time they reached a punctuation mark?

2 What does this activity reveal about Macbeth's state of mind when he wrote the letter?

3 What changes are there in the way the punctuation works though the letter?

That hast no less deserved, nor must be known 30
No less to have done so. Let me enfold thee,
And hold thee to my heart.

Banquo   There if I grow,
The harvest is your own.

Duncan   My plenteous joys,
Wanton in fulness, seek to hide themselves
In drops of sorrow. — Sons, kinsmen, thanes, 35
And you whose places are the nearest, know,
We will establish our estate upon
Our eldest, Malcolm; whom we name hereafter
The Prince of Cumberland. Which honour must
Not unaccompanied invest him only, 40
But signs of nobleness, like stars, shall shine
On all deservers. — From hence to Inverness,
And bind us further to you.

Macbeth   The rest is labour, which is not used for you.
I'll be myself the harbinger, and make joyful 45
The hearing of my wife with your approach.
So, humbly take my leave.

Duncan   My worthy Cawdor.

Macbeth   [Aside.]   The Prince of Cumberland. That is a step
On which I must fall down, or else o'erleap,
For in my way it lies. Stars hide your fires, 50
Let not light see my black and deep desires.
The eye wink at the hand: yet let that be
Which the eye fears when it is done to see.

Exit Macbeth.

Duncan   True, worthy Banquo: he is full so valiant,
And in his commendations I am fed: 55
It is a banquet to me. Let's after him,
Whose care is gone before to bid us welcome.
It is a peerless kinsman.

A fanfare of trumpets. They all exit.

ACT 1 SCENE 5

Enter Lady Macbeth, reading a letter.

Lady Macbeth   *They met me in the day of success, and I have learned by
the perfect'st report, they have more in them than mortal
knowledge. When I burned in desire to question them
further, they made themselves air, into which they vanished.
Whiles I stood rapt in the wonder of it, came missives from 5
the king, who all-hailed me 'Thane of Cawdor,' by which
title, before, these weird sisters saluted me, and referred
me to the coming on of time with 'Hail, king that shalt be!'
This have I thought good to deliver thee (my dearest partner
of greatness) that thou mightst not lose the dues of rejoicing 10
by being ignorant of what greatness is promised thee. Lay it
to thy heart, and farewell.*

30–1 **nor must be … have done so:** and people must know that is so
31 **enfold:** embrace

34 **Wanton in fulness:** growing so wildly
35 **drops of sorrow:** tears
36 **whose places are the nearest:** most closely related to Duncan

39–40 **Which honour … him only:** this will not be the only honour I give
42 **Inverness:** where Macbeth's castle is; he intends to stay there
43 **bind us further to you:** increase our debt to you
44 **The rest … used for you:** anything not done for you is hard work (this is for you, so it's no trouble)
45 **harbinger:** messenger who goes ahead to arrange places to stay

52–3 **The eye fears … done to see:** Let my eye not see what my hand is doing until it is done

54 **full so:** just as brave as you say
55 **his commendations:** praises heaped upon him

58 **peerless:** without equal

2 **perfect'st:** most reliable

5 **missives:** messengers

8 **the coming on of time:** the future
9 **deliver thee:** tell you
10 **dues of rejoicing:** chance to be glad
11–2 **Lay it to thy heart:** keep it secret

A

B

Macbeth and Lady Macbeth.

This is the first time the audience see Macbeth and Lady Macbeth together. What do these photos suggest about the different interpretations of the relationship between them in the two productions?

A: Elliot Cowan and Laura Rogers, summer 2010;
B: James Garnon and Claire Cox, spring 2010.

FROM THE REHEARSAL ROOM...

POWER WORDS

Act 1 Scene 5 starts with two soliloquies by Lady Macbeth (lines 13–28 and 36–52). Each member of the group is given one or more lines.

- Choose three words that seem most important in your line. These can be any words you like. For example, from line 13 you could choose *Glamis, Cawdor,* and *be*.
- The group reads the soliloquies out loud, each person just saying the 'power' words, not the whole line.
- Now read the soliloquies again. This time each person reads their whole line, giving special emphasis to the 'power' words.

1 What kind of words have people chosen?
2 What do these words tell us about this soliloquy?
3 What images do these words conjure up in your mind?
4 This is the first time that the audience meets Lady Macbeth. What first impression does Shakespeare give them of Lady Macbeth? Explain your answer.

Glamis thou art, and Cawdor; and shalt be
What thou art promised. Yet do I fear thy nature,
It is too full o' th' milk of human kindness   15
To catch the nearest way. Thou wouldst be great,
Art not without ambition, but without
The illness should attend it. What thou wouldst highly,
That wouldst thou holily: wouldst not play false,
And yet wouldst wrongly win. Thou'dst have, great
                                                  Glamis, 20
That which cries, 'Thus thou must do,' if thou have it:
And that which rather thou do'st fear to do
Than wishest should be undone. Hie thee hither,
That I may pour my spirits in thine ear,
And chastise with the valour of my tongue   25
All that impedes thee from the golden round,
Which fate and metaphysical aid doth seem
To have thee crown'd withal.

Enter a Messenger.

                    What is your tidings?

Messenger   The King comes here tonight.

Lady Macbeth   Thou'rt mad to say it.
Is not thy master with him? Who, were't so,   30
Would have informed for preparation.

Messenger   So please you, it is true. Our thane is coming.
One of my fellows had the speed of him,
Who, almost dead for breath, had scarcely more
Than would make up his message.

Lady Macbeth   Give him tending,   35
He brings great news.   *Exit Messenger.*
                    The raven himself is hoarse
That croaks the fatal entrance of Duncan
Under my battlements. Come you spirits
That tend on mortal thoughts, unsex me here,
And fill me from the crown to the toe, top-full   40
Of direst cruelty. Make thick my blood,
Stop up the access and passage to remorse,
That no compunctious visitings of nature
Shake my fell purpose, nor keep peace between
Th' effect and it. Come to my woman's breasts,   45
And take my milk for gall, your murd'ring ministers,
Wherever in your sightless substances
You wait on nature's mischief. Come thick night,
And pall thee in the dunnest smoke of hell,
That my keen knife see not the wound it makes,   50
Nor heaven peep through the blanket of the dark,
To cry, 'Hold, hold'.

Enter Macbeth.

Great Glamis, Worthy Cawdor,
Greater than both by the all-hail hereafter.

15 **milk of human kindness:** compassion
16 **catch the nearest way:** take the quickest route to the crown (murder)
18 **illness should attend it:** wickedness it needs to get what it wants
18–20 **What thou would … wrongly win:** You won't cheat to get what you want, but you don't mind winning unfairly
21 **if thou have it:** to get what you want
22–3 **that which rather … should be undone:** you want the murder done, but fear doing it yourself
24 **spirits:** determination
25–6 **chastise with … golden round:** crush any argument that keeps you from taking the crown
27 **metaphysical:** supernatural

29 **tidings:** news

31 **informed for preparation:** told me so I could get everything ready
33 **had the speed:** overtook

35 **Give him tending:** Look after him

39 **tend on mortal thoughts:** listen to murderous plans
39 **unsex me:** take away my womanly nature
43 **compunctious visitings of nature:** natural feelings of pity and mercy
44 **fell:** ruthless, fierce
46 **take my milk for gall:** swap my breastmilk for a bitter juice
47 **sightless substances:** invisible shapes
48 **wait on nature's mischief:** lie in wait for humans to have evil thoughts
49 **pall:** wrap (as in a burial shroud)
49 **dunnest:** darkest

54 **all-hail hereafter:** kingship

WELCOME

- Shake hands with the people in your group, saying the word 'yes' and meaning it.
- Do it again, but this time shake hands and say the word 'no' and mean it.
- Do it again, this time shake hands and say the word 'no' but you actually mean yes.
- Do it one more time and say the word 'welcome' but you mean the opposite of welcome.

1 Think about your body, eye contact, voice and gestures when you meant what you said. Describe these actions and how it felt.

2 What is different when you say one thing but mean something else?

- Read through Scene 6 from line 10 to the end.

3 Who says one thing but means another?

4 What do you think the actor(s) playing this/these character(s) might do on stage?

Director's Note, 1.5

✔ The letter tells us Macbeth's private thoughts, then Lady Macbeth tells us hers.

✔ Lady Macbeth worries that Macbeth will not be ruthless enough to take the crown, but she is determined to push him.

✔ News comes that Duncan will stay that night, and she decides this is the perfect time to murder him.

✔ Macbeth returns, and she tells him to leave the planning to her.

✔ Is Macbeth as committed to the plan as his wife?

SHAKESPEARE'S WORLD

Lady Macbeth's position in society

Women took their status in society from their husband. In the play, Macbeth was an important noble, so his wife was an important noblewoman. Women of Lady Macbeth's class managed the household. They supervised servants and managed the accounts. A large part of a woman's role was entertaining. This gave her an opportunity to demonstrate to the entire community how well she ran her household. In this scene, Lady Macbeth welcomes King Duncan into her home. Her ability to entertain guests was important to her husband's reputation and position in society. Even though these duties were important, women were always considered subordinate to men.

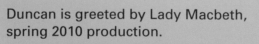

Duncan is greeted by Lady Macbeth, spring 2010 production.

Look at both actors when they were last on stage in this production (pages 18 and 22). What effect do the changes in costume have? Explain your answer.

Andrew Whipp and Claire Cox

Thy letters have transported me beyond 55
This ignorant present, and I feel now
The future in the instant.

57 **in the instant:** now

Macbeth   My dearest love,
Duncan comes here tonight.

Lady Macbeth   And when goes hence?

Macbeth   Tomorrow, as he purposes.

59 **as he purposes:** he plans

Lady Macbeth   O never
Shall sun that morrow see. 60
Your face, my thane, is as a book where men
May read strange matters. To beguile the time,
Look like the time: bear welcome in your eye,
Your hand, your tongue. Look like th' innocent flower,
But be the serpent under't. He that's coming 65
Must be provided for, and you shall put
This night's great business into my despatch,
Which shall to all our nights and days to come
Give solely sovereign sway and masterdom.

62 **beguile the time:** deceive people
63 **Look like the time:** behave normally

66 **provided for:** taken care of (in both meanings: feasted/murdered)
67 **despatch:** control, management

Macbeth   We will speak further.

Lady Macbeth   Only look up clear: 70
To alter favour ever is to fear.
Leave all the rest to me.

70 **Only look up clear:** Just behave normally
71 **To alter ... ever is to fear:** only fearful people keep changing their expressions

Exit Macbeth and Lady Macbeth.

ACT 1, SCENE 6

Enter servants with oboes and torches, followed by Duncan, Malcolm, Donalbain, Banquo, Lennox, Macduff, Ross, Angus, and Attendants.

Duncan   This castle hath a pleasant seat, the air
Nimbly and sweetly recommends itself
Unto our gentle senses.

1 **seat:** position, location

3 **gentle:** noble, well-born
4–5 **temple-haunting martlet ... wooingly here:** The swift (a bird), that nests in church walls, shows that the air is good by nesting here

Banquo   This guest of summer,
The temple-haunting martlet does approve,
By his loved mansionry, that the heaven's breath 5
Smells wooingly here. No jutty, frieze,
Buttress, nor coign of vantage, but this bird
Hath made his pendant bed and procreant cradle.
Where they most breed and haunt, I have observed
The air is delicate. 10

6–7 **jutty, frieze, Buttress, nor coign of vantage:** stonework that sticks out from the main wall
8 **pendant bed and procreant cradle:** nest and cradle for its young

Enter Lady Macbeth.

Duncan   See, see, our honoured hostess.
The love that follows us sometime is our trouble,
Which still we thank as love. Herein I teach you,
How you shall bid God yield us for your pains,
And thank us for your trouble.

12–5 **The love that follows ... for your trouble:** I'm concerned by the trouble you are going to for me, but I know it is from duty and love and will reward it.

Lady Macbeth   All our service 15
In every point twice done, and then done double,

A

B

Macbeth, from the summer 2010 production.

Which of these two photographs do you think shows Macbeth during the soliloquy (lines 1–28)? Quote from the text to support your answer.

Elliot Cowan

Director's Note, 1.6

✔ Duncan arrives to stay at Macbeth's castle.
✔ Lady Macbeth greets him, and they exchange compliments.
✔ The audience knows that Lady Macbeth is actually planning Duncan's murder. What effect does this have on how the audience views the scene?

FROM THE REHEARSAL ROOM...

POWER WORDS

Each member of the group is given one line of the soliloquy (lines 1–28).

- Choose the word that seems most important in your line. This can be any word you like, and it is often the one that jumps out at you as you first read the line.
- Read the soliloquy from lines 1–28, each person just saying the power word, not the whole line.
- Now read the soliloquy again. This time each person reads their whole line, giving special emphasis to the power word.

1 What kind of words have people chosen?
2 How do the words change as the soliloquy goes on?
3 Are there words not chosen as 'power' words that you think are more important in the soliloquy?
4 What might the 'power' words tell you about Macbeth's thoughts and feelings at the beginning, middle and end of the soliloquy?
5 How does Shakespeare show Macbeth changing through this soliloquy?

MACBETH ON THE LINE

- This is a repeat of the activity on page 14 and page 20.
- This time, do the activity and update the graph showing how likely Macbeth is to kill the king at the end of his soliloquy (line 28).

Were poor and single business to contend
Against those honours deep and broad wherewith
Your majesty loads our house. For those of old,
And the late dignities heaped up to them,   20
We rest your hermits.

Duncan   Where's the Thane of Cawdor?
We coursed him at the heels, and had a purpose
To be his purveyor. But he rides well,
And his great love (sharp as his spur) hath holp him
To his home before us. Fair and noble hostess   25
We are your guest tonight.

Lady Macbeth   Your servants ever
Have theirs, themselves, and what is theirs, in compt,
To make their audit at your highness' pleasure,
Still to return your own.

Duncan   Give me your hand.
Conduct me to mine host, we love him highly,   30
And shall continue our graces towards him.
By your leave, hostess.

They all exit.

ACT 1, SCENE 7: A room in Macbeth's castle.

*Enter servants with oboes and torches. They are followed by
the Steward, and more servants carrying dishes and food.
They cross the stage, and exit.*

Then enter Macbeth.

Macbeth   If it were done, when 'tis done, then 'twere well
It were done quickly. If th' assassination
Could trammel up the consequence, and catch
With his surcease, success: that but this blow
Might be the be-all and the end-all. Here,   5
But here, upon this bank and shoal of time,
We'd jump the life to come. But in these cases,
We still have judgement here, that we but teach
Bloody instructions, which being taught, return
To plague th' inventor. This even-handed justice   10
Commends th' ingredients of our poisoned chalice
To our own lips. He's here in double trust:
First, as I am his kinsman, and his subject,
Strong both against the deed. Then, as his host,
Who should against his murderer shut the door,   15
Not bear the knife myself. Besides, this Duncan
Hath borne his faculties so meek, hath been
So clear in his great office, that his virtues
Will plead like angels, trumpet-tongued against
The deep damnation of his taking-off.   20
And Pity, like a naked new-born babe,
Striding the blast, or heaven's cherubin, horsed
Upon the sightless couriers of the air,
Shall blow the horrid deed in every eye,

17 **single business:** feeble effort
17-8 **to contend Against:** compared to
19 **those of old:** honours you have given us in the past
20 **late dignities heaped up:** more recent ones
21 **rest your hermits:** will constantly thank you, as medieval hermits constantly pray for others
22 **coursed:** chased
22-3 **had a purpose ... his purveyor:** hoped to get here first to announce his coming

27 **in compt ... highness' pleasure:** from you, in trust, always ready to return it

32 **By your leave:** Shall we go in?

1 **If it were done, when 'tis done:** (Macbeth is talking about killing Duncan)
2-4 **If th' assassination ... success:** If the murder was certain to make me king without further trouble
6 **bank and shoal of time:** in our short life on earth (compared to eternity)
7 **jump the life to come:** risk punishment in the afterlife
8-10 **that we but teach ... th' inventor:** we set others the example of violence which is then turned against us
11-2 **Commends ... our own lips:** makes us drink from our own cup of poison
12 **He's here in double trust:** he has two reasons to trust me
17-8 **borne his faculties ... great office:** has been such a good and generous king
20 **taking-off:** murder
22 **the blast:** the outcry at the murder
23 **sightless couriers of the air:** winds

Macbeth and Lady Macbeth argue in this scene, from the summer 2010 production.

Which line do you think was being spoken when this photo was taken? Quote to support your answer.

Elliot Cowan and Laura Rogers

Working cut - text for experiment

Lady M	Was the hope drunk,
	Wherein you dressed yourself? Hath it slept since?
Mac	Pr'ythee, peace!
	I dare do all that may become a man,
Lady M	What beast was't, then
	That made you break this enterprise to me?
Mac	If we should fail?
Lady M	We fail?
	But screw your courage to the sticking-place,
	And we'll not fail.
	What cannot you and I perform upon
	Th' unguarded Duncan?
Mac	Bring forth men-children only,
	Will it not be received,
	When we have marked with blood those sleepy two
	Of his own chamber, and used their very daggers,
	That they have done't?
Lady M	Who dares receive it other,
Mac	I am settled.

That tears shall drown the wind. I have no spur
To prick the sides of my intent, but only
Vaulting ambition, which o'erleaps itself,
And falls on th' other.

Enter Lady Macbeth.

How now? What news?

Lady Macbeth He has almost supped. Why have you left the chamber?

Macbeth Hath he asked for me?

Lady Macbeth   Know you not he has?

Macbeth We will proceed no further in this business.
He hath honoured me of late, and I have bought
Golden opinions from all sorts of people,
Which would be worn now in their newest gloss,
Not cast aside so soon.

Lady Macbeth   Was the hope drunk,
Wherein you dressed yourself? Hath it slept since?
And wakes it now, to look so green and pale
At what it did so freely? From this time,
Such I account thy love. Art thou afeard
To be the same in thine own act and valour,
As thou art in desire? Wouldst thou have that
Which thou esteem'st the ornament of life,
And live a coward in thine own esteem?
Letting 'I dare not' wait upon 'I would,'
Like the poor cat i' th' adage?

Macbeth   Pr'ythee, peace!
I dare do all that may become a man,
Who dares do more, is none.

Lady Macbeth   What beast was't, then
That made you break this enterprise to me?
When you durst do it, then you were a man:
And to be more than what you were, you would
Be so much more the man. Nor time, nor place
Did then adhere, and yet you would make both.
They have made themselves, and that their fitness now
Does unmake you. I have given suck, and know
How tender 'tis to love the babe that milks me —
I would, while it was smiling in my face,
Have plucked my nipple from his boneless gums,
And dashed the brains out, had I so sworn as you
Have done to this.

Macbeth   If we should fail?

Lady Macbeth   We fail?
But screw your courage to the sticking-place,
And we'll not fail. When Duncan is asleep,
(Whereto the rather shall his day's hard journey
Soundly invite him) his two chamberlains
Will I with wine and wassail so convince,

---

25 |
27 |

25–6 spur To prick … my intent: nothing to drive me to act
27 o'erleaps: jumps too high

30 |

32 of late: recently
32–3 bought Golden opinions: earned a high reputation
34 would: should
34 newest gloss: while it is new
35–6 Was the hope … dressed yourself?: Were your earlier plans made while drunk on ambition?
37 green and pale: hung over
39 account: value
40–1 To be the same … art in desire?: to act bravely to get the thing you want
42 the ornament of life: the high reputation you value so much
43 live a coward … esteem: live with the fact you see yourself as a coward
45 cat i' th' adage: the adage (proverb) is 'the cat wanted fish, but would not get her paws wet'
45 Pr'ythee, peace!: For heaven's sake stop pushing me!
46 may become: is suitable; is proper behaviour for
47 is none: is not a proper man
49 durst: dared to
51–2 Nor time … make both: Neither the time nor the place were right then, yet you said you wished they were, so you could act
53–4 They have … unmake you: Now the time and place *are* right, it has made you fearful of acting
54 given suck: breastfed a baby
58 had I so sworn: if I had made such a solemn promise
59 this: the killing of Duncan
60 screw … sticking place: be brave, don't waver
62–3 (Whereto … him): Which he's likely to do deeply after his hard journey
63 chamberlains: servants who put the king to bed, get him up and guard him while he sleeps
64 with wine … so convince: get so drunk

35 |
40 |
45 |
50 |
55 |
60 |

29

A

B

C

Macbeth and Lady Macbeth during this scene from the 2001 production.

1 Which order do you think the three photos were taken in this scene? Give reasons for your answer.

2 Pick one line from the scene to be the caption for each photo and give reasons for your answer.

Jasper Britton and Eve Best

Director's Note, 1.7

✔ Macbeth thinks about the plan to murder Duncan, and decides not to do it.

✔ Lady Macbeth is angry at his change of plan, argues with him, and persuades him they should go ahead and murder Duncan.

✔ The balance of power shifts between Macbeth and Lady Macbeth. What are the shifts and which key lines show them?

The photo opposite is from the Globe's summer 2010 production (directed by Lucy Bailey).

In this scene she chose to have Duncan and the nobles on stage. They are at the back of the stage, drinking and quietly singing drinking songs, while Macbeth's soliloquy and the dialogue with Lady Macbeth happen on the front of the stage.

Why might she have made this choice?

That memory, the warder of the brain, 65
Shall be a fume, and the receipt of reason
A limbeck only. When in swinish sleep
Their drenchéd natures lie as in a death,
What cannot you and I perform upon
Th' unguarded Duncan? What not put upon 70
His spongy officers, who shall bear the guilt
Of our great quell?

Macbeth Bring forth men-children only,
For thy undaunted mettle should compose
Nothing but males. Will it not be received, 75
When we have marked with blood those sleepy two
Of his own chamber, and used their very daggers,
That they have done't?

Lady Macbeth Who dares receive it other,
As we shall make our griefs and clamour roar
Upon his death?

Macbeth I am settled, and bend up 80
Each corporal agent to this terrible feat.
Away, and mock the time with fairest show,
False face must hide what the false heart doth know.

Exit Both.

66 **receipt of reason:** brain
67 **limbeck:** a container alcohol passes through in the distilling process

70 **put upon:** blame
71 **spongy officers:** the drunken servants
72 **quell:** murder
74 **undaunted mettle:** fearless nature

75 **received:** believed

78 **other:** in any other way

80–1 **I am settled ... terrible feat:** I'm decided and focusing my whole being on this horrible act
82 **mock the time ... show:** behave normally to deceive everyone

EXAMINER'S NOTES, 1.7

These questions help you to explore many aspects of *Macbeth*. At GCSE, your teacher will tell you which aspects are relevant to how your Shakespeare response will be assessed.

1 Character and plot development

So far, Macbeth has been presented as a strong leader and soldier, highly praised for bravery and ruthlessness. This view is created by how others speak about him. Now we have an insight into what he is like in private where we see him changeable. So far Lady Macbeth is shown as a woman who thinks she understands her husband well and has ideas about what he is like if left to his own devices. Her view of him has not been the same as the other, male, military characters.

1   What does the scene add to our understanding of Macbeth as a man with good and evil in his character? Pick words that show he has a conscience and that show elements of evil in his character.

2   In what ways does Shakespeare use the scene to show the relationship between Macbeth and Lady Macbeth? Which partner appears to be more dominant? Explain your answer with examples.

3   How does the scene create audience sympathy and disapproval for Macbeth and for Lady Macbeth? What are your reactions to them? Refer closely to the text to support your opinions.

2 Characterisation and voice: dramatic language

Voice is an important part of character, on stage. What we hear tells us as much as what we see. Shakespeare's stage had no sound amplification. His Macbeth had to be heard in an open-air theatre even when he is apparently whispering. Shakespeare lets us understand motives and feelings by building a speech to show us the drama of conflict within the person. We hear in Macbeth's words his motives and doubts as he comes to a decision, building up to his action on stage.

4   How is Macbeth feeling in the first four lines of the soliloquy? What repetition of sounds does Shakespeare use to suggest this?

5   How does Shakespeare draw on his audience's familiarity with horses to convey two ideas in the last four lines of the soliloquy?

6   How does Shakespeare show the tension within Macbeth as he considers the murder? How does he make Duncan's virtues seem like strengths against his killer?

3 Themes and ideas

The scene shows that Macbeth can't get out of his head ideas to do with morality, loyalty, duty and God's Judgment. Lady Macbeth puts up different kinds of ideas, such as courage, self-esteem and manliness.

7   How does Macbeth's feeling of loyalty to Duncan link with anything we know he has done so far in the play; e.g. in battle?

8   How does his fear of justice in 'the life to come' link with any other references to God, Heaven or Judgement here or earlier?

9   Why might Lady Macbeth make such an issue about manliness? What feelings and reaction might she hope to provoke in Macbeth?

10 How does Lady Macbeth's understanding of how to change his mind link with anything earlier in the play; e.g. Act 1 Scene 5?

EXAMINER'S TIP

Voice

A character may speak in many different ways according to who they are speaking to, and how they feel. A character's language may show signs of attitude or of feeling, so that an audience can tell if the character is worried, angry, curious, challenging or trying to persuade.

Voice is the kind of speech behaviour which is so typical of a character that an audience can recognise who is speaking from a small extract. This may be because of accent, dialect or a personal language habit.

For example, Macbeth:
'Pr'ythee, peace! dare do all that may become a man, Who dares do more, is none' 1.7.45–7 (Confident, proud and in control)

'If we should fail?' 1.7.59 (Doubting, hesitant and needing reassurance)

'I am settled, and bend up/Each corporal agent to this terrible feat.' 1.7.80–1 (Firm, determined and aware of what he is doing)

EXAMINER'S NOTES, 1.7

4 Performance

The way the two characters speak to each other is important. They may use tones of voice that are harsh, cajoling, encouraging or scornful. Their gestures, too, will matter. They may point, jab, tug, embrace or stroke to reinforce their spoken impact on each other.

11 At which point may Macbeth try not to look directly at his wife? Explain your answer with a suitable quote.

12 At which point might Lady Macbeth move into a position where Macbeth had to look her straight in the face? What would you suggest Lady Macbeth should do with her hands at this moment? (e.g. make a fist, reach out to Macbeth?) Quote from the text to support your answer.

13 How might you bring out the most important aspects of this scene if you were directing it for a) stage performance and b) filmed performance?

5 Contexts and responses

Audiences in different times and places may react differently to Shakespeare's characters, themes and ideas. Some may have been more important to Shakespeare's audience but others may be as important today. Audiences may prefer watching a hero being heroic, a villain being villainous or a hero turning into a villain. You may have your own preferences and view of what is more true to life.

14 Which of Macbeth's reasons for not going ahead do you think would be most powerful today? Why?

15 Why do you think Macbeth, who could kill enemies in battle, finds it hard to kill Duncan under his own roof?

16 Which one of Lady Macbeth's tactics do you think an audience in Shakespeare's time would find most shocking? Why?

17 Which one of her tactics do you think a modern audience would find least shocking? Why?

6 Reflecting on the scene

18 How does Shakespeare present differences between the characters of Macbeth and Lady Macbeth by what they say? Look at what they say and how they say it.

19 How does Shakespeare make Macbeth's and Lady Macbeth's different feelings and ideas interesting to watch in action on stage?

20 Explain how your reading of the text and viewing of performances helps you to understand that audiences might have different interpretations and sympathies in response to this scene.

USING THE VIDEO

Exploring interpretation and performance

If you have looked at the video extracts in the online version try these questions.

- One of the performances shows the dinner guests on stage. What difference does this make to the argument between Macbeth and Lady Macbeth?

- One of the performances shows very little close contact between the two until they go off, and a lot of space between them. How does this affect the way they speak and act?

Banquo, Fleance and Macbeth in the summer 2010 production.

1 What is happening on stage?

2 Why might the director have chosen to stage the scene like this?

l–r Christian Bradley, James Beesley, Elliot Cowan

FROM THE REHEARSAL ROOM...

WHAT I SAY AND WHAT I THINK

- In pairs, read lines 23–38. One read Banquo, and the other Macbeth.

- After you have read your lines, say in your own words what you think your character is really thinking. Is it the same as what you just read?

1 What does this activity tell you about Banquo and Macbeth, and their relationship at this point in the play?

SHAKESPEARE'S WORLD

Stage directions in the text

Shakespeare often suggests what actors could do in the lines the characters speak. When Banquo says, 'Hold, take my sword', it is clear he is offering his sword to Fleance. However, what does Banquo offer to Fleance when he says, 'Take thou that, too'? In the Globe in 1606, actors could ask Shakespeare what he meant. Today, it is up to directors and actors. Some choose Banquo's cloak, others choose the diamond he has to give to Lady Macbeth (see line 17). You will find plenty more examples as you read on.

ACT 2 SCENE 1

Enter Fleance carrying a torch, followed by Banquo.

Banquo How goes the night, boy?

Fleance The moon is down, I have not heard the clock.

Banquo And she goes down at twelve.

Fleance I take't 'tis later, sir.

Banquo Hold, take my sword.   5
There's husbandry in heaven,
Their candles are all out. Take thee that too.
A heavy summons lies like lead upon me,
And yet I would not sleep.
Merciful powers, restrain in me the cursed thoughts
that nature   10
Gives way to in repose.

Enter a servant carrying a torch, and Macbeth.

Give me my sword. Who's there?

Macbeth A friend.

Banquo What sir, not yet at rest? The king's abed.
He hath been in unusual pleasure, and   15
Sent forth great largess to your offices.

Giving Macbeth a diamond.

This diamond he greets your wife withal,
By the name of most kind hostess, and shut up
In measureless content.

Macbeth Being unprepared,   20
Our will became the servant to defect,
Which else should free have wrought.

Banquo All's well.
I dreamt last night of the three weird sisters.
To you they have showed some truth.   25

Macbeth I think not of them.
Yet, when we can entreat an hour to serve,
We would spend it in some words upon that business,
If you would grant the time.

Banquo At your kind'st leisure.   30

Macbeth If you shall cleave to my consent, when 'tis,
It shall make honour for you.

Banquo So I lose none
In seeking to augment it, but still keep
My bosom franchised, and allegiance clear,   35
I shall be counselled.

Macbeth Good repose the while.

Banquo Thanks, sir. The like to you.

Exit Banquo and Fleance.

---

2 **down:** set

6 **husbandry:** careful housekeeping

7 **candles:** stars

8-9 **A heavy summons ... not sleep:** my body is begging me to sleep, but I don't want to

10-1 **nature Gives way to in repose:** come to mind when I rest

15-6 **He hath ... your offices:** He's enjoyed himself hugely and sent the servants money as a reward

18 **shut up:** gone to bed

20-2 **Being unprepared ... have wrought:** The suddenness of his arrival meant we could not do as much as we would have liked

27 **entreat an hour to serve:** can make some time

30 **At your kind'st leisure:** When it suits you

31 **shall cleave ...when 'tis:** will follow my advice when we do talk

33-4 **So I lose ... augment it:** As long as I don't have to do something dishonourable to get the honours you promise

35 **My bosom ... allegiance clear:** my conscience and duty to the king

36 **I shall be counselled:** I'll take your advice

37 **Good repose the while:** Sleep well!

Macbeth and the three Witches during the soliloquy, summer 2010.

1 The text does not have Witches on stage at this point. Why might the director of this production have chosen to include them in this scene?

2 Which line from the soliloquy was being spoken when this photo was taken? Give reasons for your answer.

FROM THE REHEARSAL ROOM...

IAMBIC PENTAMETERS

- Shakespeare often used the rhythm of the iambic pentameter in his plays. This is ten syllables, or two beats, repeated five times. 'Sha-boom' is a good way to illustrate the rhythm of two beats.
- As a whole group repeat 'Sha-boom' five times and clap on the syllables.
- Repeat the activity. This time replace 'Sha-boom' with the first two lines spoken by Macbeth on page 37. Some lines don't fit – they are longer or shorter.
- Draw three parallel lines on a sheet of paper. Read and clap through Macbeth's soliloquy (lines 41–69). For each line mark an X on the middle line if it has ten beats, on the higher line if it has more, and on the lower if it has less. Join up your marks.

1 What does this chart tell us about Macbeth's feelings?

2 What might Shakespeare be asking his actors to do when there are fewer than ten syllables?

Director's Note, 2.1

✔ Banquo and Macbeth meet. They are no longer easy with each other. Banquo speaks about the Witches' prophecies.

✔ Macbeth pretends to have forgotten them, but then seems to ask for Banquo's support.

✔ Banquo makes it clear he will always be loyal to Duncan.

✔ Left alone, Macbeth imagines he sees a dagger leading him to Duncan's room.

✔ What impression of Macbeth's mental state does Shakespeare create by the vision of the dagger?

Macbeth   Go bid thy mistress, when my drink is ready,
She strike upon the bell. Get thee to bed.   40

Exit Servant.

Is this a dagger which I see before me,
The handle toward my hand? Come, let me clutch thee.
I have thee not, and yet I see thee still.
Art thou not, fatal vision, sensible
To feeling as to sight? Or art thou but   45
A dagger of the mind, a false creation,
Proceeding from the heat-oppressèd brain?
I see thee yet, in form as palpable
As this which now I draw.   *[Drawing his dagger.]*
Thou marshall'st me the way that I was going,   50
And such an instrument I was to use.
Mine eyes are made the fools o' th' other senses,
Or else worth all the rest. I see thee still;
And on thy blade and dudgeon gouts of blood,
Which was not so before. There's no such thing.   55
It is the bloody business which informs
Thus to mine eyes. Now o'er the one-half world
Nature seems dead, and wicked dreams abuse
The curtained sleep. Witchcraft celebrates
Pale Hecate's offerings: and withered murder,   60
Alarumed by his sentinel, the wolf,
Whose howl's his watch, thus with his stealthy pace,
With Tarquin's ravishing strides, towards his design
Moves like a ghost. Thou sure and firm-set earth,
Hear not my steps, which way they walk, for fear   65
Thy very stones prate of my whereabout,
And take the present horror from the time,
Which now suits with it. Whiles I threat, he lives:
Words to the heat of deeds too cold breath gives.

A bell rings.

I go, and it is done. The bell invites me.   70
Hear it not, Duncan, for it is a knell,
That summons thee to heaven, or to hell.

Exit.

ACT 2 SCENE 2

Enter Lady Macbeth.

Lady Macbeth   That which hath made them drunk hath made me bold.
What hath quenched them hath given me fire.
Hark! Peace. It was the owl that shrieked,
The fatal bellman, which gives the stern'st good night. —
He is about it. The doors are open,   5
And the surfeited grooms do mock their charge
With snores. I have drugg'd their possets,
That death and nature do contend about them,
Whether they live or die.

43 have thee not: can't take hold of you
44–5 sensible To feeling … sight?: able to be touched as well as seen?
47 heat-oppressèd: fevered
48 palpable: solid, touchable
50 marshall'st: directs
52–3 Mine … all the rest: Either my eyes or my other senses are lying to me
54 dudgeon: handle
56–7 bloody business … mine eyes: thinking of murder that makes me see this
58 abuse: disturb
60 Hecate: goddess of the moon and witchcraft
61 Alarumed: called to act
61 sentinel: sentry, guard
62 Whose howl's his watch: who howls regularly, as a watchman calls out that all is well
63 Tarquin: Sextus Tarquinius, son of a Roman ruler, who raped the wife of a noble Roman (she then killed herself)
63 ravishing: raping
66 prate: tell of
67–8 take the present … with it: break the horrifying silence of the night, which suits my plans
68 Whiles I threat, he lives: While I just threaten murder, Duncan still lives
69 Words to the heat … breath gives: Too much talking cools the hot urge to act
71 knell: funeral bell

2 quenched: put them to sleep
4 fatal bellman: person who rings a bell outside the cell of a prisoner the night before he is executed
4 stern'st: harshest
5 He is about it: Macbeth's committing the murder
6–7 surfeited … snores: men who should be guarding Duncan are drunk and snoring
7 possets: hot drinks of milk mixed with alcohol
8–9 That death … live or die: so heavily that they may die

Macbeth from the 2001 production.

This production created and used its own world of symbols. What might the golden straw represent? Give reasons for your answer.

Jasper Britton

FROM THE REHEARSAL ROOM...

OVERLAPS AND PAUSES

- Get into pairs. One of you read the part of Macbeth and the other read the part of Lady Macbeth.
- As you read through the scene, you must start saying your lines two or three words before your partner has finished speaking so that your lines will overlap.

1 How does the overlapping affect the action in this scene? Does it work? If so, why?

2 What does the rhythm of the scene, and the iambic pentameter, tell actors today about how Shakespeare might have imagined this scene?

3 What does this bring to the relationship between Macbeth and Lady Macbeth in this situation?

- Read through the scene again, except this time you must count three seconds in your head before you start saying your lines so that you have a three second pause between each section of dialogue.

4 How did the pausing affect the scene? In what ways is this different to overlapping?

5 How does interrupting or pausing affect the audience's interpretation of the relationship between Macbeth and Lady Macbeth?

6 Which way works best for you and your interpretation of the scene?

Enter Macbeth, unseen by Lady Macbeth, and carrying two bloody daggers.

Macbeth	Who's there? What ho?	10

Lady Macbeth Alack, I am afraid they have awaked,
And 'tis not done. Th' attempt and not the deed
Confounds us. Hark! I laid their daggers ready,
He could not miss 'em. Had he not resembled
My father as he slept, I had done't.   15
My husband?

Macbeth I have done the deed.
Didst thou not hear a noise?

Lady Macbeth I heard the owl scream and the crickets cry.
Did not you speak?   20

Macbeth When?

Lady Macbeth Now.

Macbeth As I descended?

Lady Macbeth Ay.

Macbeth Hark! — Who lies i' th' second chamber?   25

Lady Macbeth Donalbain.

Macbeth This is a sorry sight.

Lady Macbeth A foolish thought, to say a sorry sight.

Macbeth There's one did laugh in's sleep,
And one cried, 'Murder!' That they did wake each other.   30
I stood and heard them. But they did say their prayers,
And addressed them again to sleep.

Lady Macbeth There are two lodged together.

Macbeth One cried, 'God bless us' and, 'Amen' the other,
As they had seen me with these hangman's hands.   35
Listening their fear, I could not say 'Amen,'
When they did say, 'God bless us.'

Lady Macbeth Consider it not so deeply.

Macbeth But wherefore could not I pronounce 'Amen'?
I had most need of blessing, and 'Amen'   40
Stuck in my throat.

Lady Macbeth   These deeds must not be thought
After these ways: so, it will make us mad.

Macbeth Methought I heard a voice cry, 'Sleep no more.
Macbeth does murder sleep.' The innocent sleep:
Sleep that knits up the ravelled sleeve of care,   45
The death of each day's life, sore labour's bath,
Balm of hurt minds, great nature's second course,
Chief nourisher in life's feast.

12–3 **Th' attempt ... Confounds us:** We'll be caught in the attempt and ruined before we can commit the deed

15 **I had done't:** I would have done it

27 **This is a sorry sight:** referring to the bloodstains on him

30 **That:** so

32 **addressed them again to sleep:** went back to sleep

33 **lodged together:** sleeping in the same room

35 **As:** as if

39 **wherefore could I not pronounce:** why couldn't I say

42 **After:** in

42 **so:** if we do so

45 **knits up ... sleeve of care:** uses knitting imagery to say that sleep calms the mind

46 **sore labour's bath:** the warm bath that soothes the aches of the day's work

47 **balm:** soothing influence on

47 **great nature's second course:** the main, most important, part of a meal (so the most important part of life)

A

Macbeth and Lady Macbeth from the summer 2010 production.

1 Which of these two photos was taken first? Give reasons for your answer.

2 Pick a line which would make a good caption for each photo, and explain your answer.

Elliot Cowan and Laura Rogers

B

Actor's view

Claire Cox – talking about killing Duncan Lady Macbeth, spring 2010

At the time, she perhaps feels like it's a sign of weakness in herself. But it is a sign of humanity, because it's a sign that she can talk about it and tell Macbeth that he's got to do it, but when it comes to it herself, she can't really do it. She can't actually do the deed herself. To actually physically do something like that is too terrifying and there was a vulnerability about him, this older man, perhaps who really does look a bit like her father. Throughout her life she would have leant a lot on men, probably especially her father, and it would have seemed very strange to have then destroyed that. So I think it is a sign of humanity but she feels at the time that it's a sign of weakness.

Director's Note, 2.2

✔ Lady Macbeth waits for Macbeth while he kills Duncan.

✔ Macbeth is horrified by what he has done, and he has spoilt the plan, by not leaving the daggers he used next to the grooms.

✔ Macbeth will not take the daggers back, so Lady Macbeth takes control – she does take them back.

✔ Somebody knocks at the castle gate. Lady Macbeth urges Macbeth to wash the blood off and change.

✔ Who is the dominant partner in this scene?

Lady Macbeth	What do you mean?
Macbeth	Still it cried, 'Sleep no more' to all the house. 50 'Glamis hath murdered sleep, and therefore Cawdor Shall sleep no more. Macbeth shall sleep no more.'
Lady Macbeth	Who was it that thus cried? Why, worthy thane, You do unbend your noble strength, to think So brainsickly of things. Go get some water, 55 And wash this filthy witness from your hand.

[She sees the daggers].

Why did you bring these daggers from the place?
They must lie there. Go carry them, and smear
The sleepy grooms with blood.

Macbeth	I'll go no more. I am afraid to think what I have done. 60 Look on't again, I dare not.
Lady Macbeth	Infirm of purpose! Give me the daggers. The sleeping and the dead Are but as pictures. 'Tis the eye of childhood That fears a painted devil. If he do bleed, 65 I'll gild the faces of the grooms withal, For it must seem their guilt.

Exit Lady Macbeth. A loud knocking, off stage.

Macbeth	Whence is that knocking? How is't with me, when every noise appals me? What hands are here? Ha, they pluck out mine eyes. 70 Will all great Neptune's ocean wash this blood Clean from my hand? No. This my hand will rather The multitudinous seas incarnadine, Making the green one red.

Enter Lady Macbeth, [with bloody hands].

Lady Macbeth	My hands are of your colour, but I shame 75 To wear a heart so white. *A loud knocking, within.* I hear a knocking at the south entry. Retire we to our chamber. A little water clears us of this deed. How easy is it then! Your constancy 80 Hath left you unattended *More loud knocking, within.* Hark, more knocking: Get on your nightgown, lest occasion call us And show us to be watchers. — Be not lost So poorly in your thoughts. 85
Macbeth	To know my deed, *More loud knocking, within.* 'Twere best not know myself. Wake Duncan with thy knocking. I would thou couldst.

Exit Macbeth and Lady Macbeth.

---

54 **unbend:** weaken
55 **brainsickly:** frantically, madly
56 **filthy witness:** bloody evidence of your crime

62 **Infirm of purpose!:** Weak-willed man!
64–5 **but as pictures … painted devil:** like 'scary' pictures that only children would fear
66 **gild:** smear
66 **withal:** at the same time as leaving the daggers
67 **seem:** suggest
68 **Whence … knocking?:** Where's that knocking coming from?
70 **What hands … eyes?:** I want to pull out my eyes so I can't see the bloodstains on my hands
71 **Neptune:** god of the sea
72–4 **This my hand … one red:** instead, my bloodstained hands will dye the green seas red

75–6 **I shame … so white:** I would be ashamed if I was a cowardly as you

80–1 **Your … unattended:** your self-control has deserted you
83–4 **lest … watchers:** in case people call us and see we have not been asleep in our beds

85 **so poorly:** in such a cowardly way

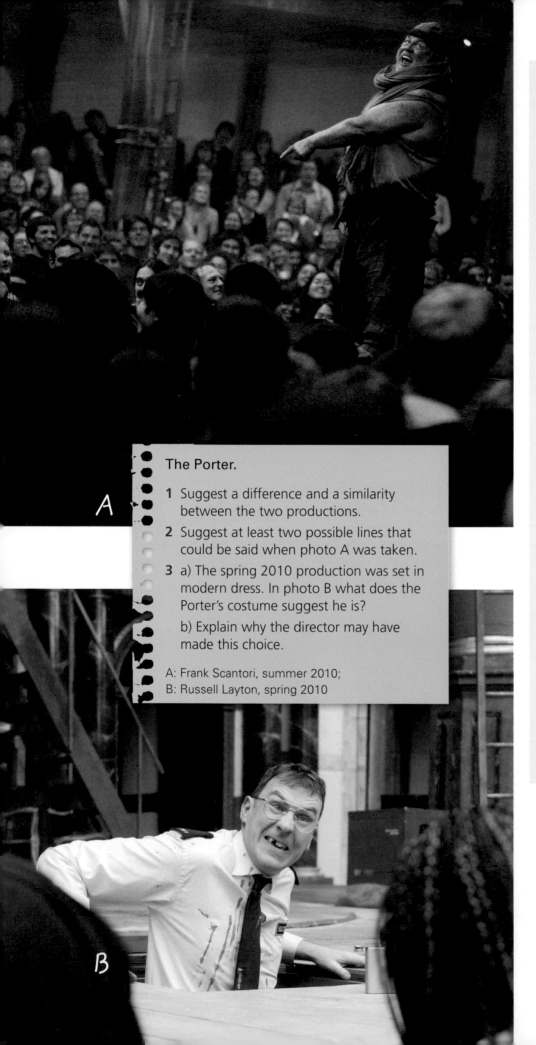

A

The Porter.

1 Suggest a difference and a similarity between the two productions.

2 Suggest at least two possible lines that could be said when photo A was taken.

3 a) The spring 2010 production was set in modern dress. In photo B what does the Porter's costume suggest he is?

b) Explain why the director may have made this choice.

A: Frank Scantori, summer 2010;
B: Russell Layton, spring 2010

B

Director's view

Bill Buckhurst
Director, spring 2010

[At the end of the murder scene] the stage is left empty for a moment, with the audience absolutely with their hearts in their mouths, having seen this gruesomeness.

And then the Porter arrives to answer the door, and in our production he comes up through a trap, as if his office is below stairs. What happens is the audience have their hearts in their mouths and Lady Macbeth and Macbeth leave and there's a few moments as the knocking goes on, and there's this 'BANG!' of the trap opening, which gives everyone a shock … which is quite nice! And interesting to see the audience respond to that as their nerves are on edge.

I think it's a brilliantly structured bit of storytelling. Just at the moment when the audience are wrung out, strung out and have been thrown around the place by the storytelling and the tension which has been built up, on comes this guy who cracks a few jokes. It's a bit of comic relief for us to gather ourselves before the story continues.

And it works terribly well as it gives a little bit of respite after this very intense story which has been taken to a real climactic point. We almost forget about the story for a moment, and then Macduff arrives with Lennox, and we're straight back into it. Also, it gives enough time for the actor playing Macbeth to get clean! We did do a bit of research on how much blood [there would be] if you hit a major artery – there's going to be a lot of blood, it's going to be everywhere, pints and pints of blood all over him. So he had it on his shirt, on his face, on his hands, and he needs time to get changed, to get rid of the evidence, so he can come in completely calmly.

ACT 2 SCENE 3

Enter a Porter.

More loud knocking within.

Porter   Here's a knocking indeed. If a man were porter of hell gate, he should have old turning the key.

More loud knocking within.

Knock, knock, knock. Who's there, i' the name of Belzebub? Here's a farmer, that hanged himself on th' expectation of plenty. Come in time, have napkins enough about you, here you'll sweat for't.   5

More loud knocking off stage.

Knock, knock. Who's there in th' other devil's name? Faith, here's an equivocator, that could swear in both the scales against either scale, who committed treason enough for God's sake, yet could not equivocate to heaven. O come in, equivocator.   10

More loud knocking within.

Knock, knock, knock! Who's there? Faith, here's an English tailor come hither, for stealing out of a French hose. Come in tailor, here you may roast your goose.

More loud knocking within.

Knock, knock. Never at quiet. What are you? — But this place is too cold for hell. I'll devil-porter it no further. I had thought to have let in some of all professions that go the primrose way to the everlasting bonfire.   15

More loud knocking within.

Anon, anon! I pray you, remember the porter.

[He opens the door. Enter Macduff and Lennox.]

Macduff   Was it so late, friend, ere you went to bed,   20
That you do lie so late?

Porter   Faith, sir, we were carousing till the second cock, and drink, sir, is a great provoker of three things.

Macduff   What three things does drink especially provoke?

Porter   Marry, sir, nose-painting, sleep, and urine. Lechery, sir,   25
it provokes and unprovokes. It provokes the desire, but it takes away the performance. Therefore much drink may be said to be an equivocator with lechery. It makes him, and it mars him; it sets him on, and it takes him off; it persuades him, and disheartens him; makes him   30
stand to, and not stand to. In conclusion, equivocates him in a sleep, and giving him the lie, leaves him.

Macduff   I believe drink gave thee the lie last night.

Porter   That it did, sir, i' the very throat on me. But I requited him for his lie, and (I think) being too strong for him,   35
though he took up my legs sometime, yet I made a shift to cast him.

2 **have old:** plenty of
4 **Belzebub:** the devil
5 **th' expectation of plenty:** when a good harvest was predicted (so he couldn't charge as much)
5 **Come in time:** you've come at the right time
6 **napkins:** handkerchiefs (to mop up the sweat)
8 **equivocator:** someone who deliberately says things that can be understood in different ways
8-11 **that could swear … heaven:** that could argue each side of an argument so well that the scales of Justice were balanced, but who could not talk his way into heaven
13-4 **stealing out … hose:** French hose (cloth leggings or stockings) were wide, English ones less so. The porter is accusing the tailor of re-shaping French hose, to steal the extra fabric.
14 **roast your goose:** heat your tailor's iron (called 'goose' because of its shape)
18 **primrose way … bonfire:** attractive-looking, sinful, path to hell
19 **remember:** remember to tip – give money for the services of
20 **ere:** before
22 **carousing till the second cock:** drinking until three in the morning
23 **is a great provoker of:** often sets off
25 **Marry:** By the Virgin Mary, used at the start of a sentence for emphasis as 'Well' can be now
25 **nose-painting:** getting a red nose (through drinking too much)
25 **Lechery:** lust, sexual desire
27-31 **It makes him … not stand to:** the rest of the speech keeps contrasting the way drink makes a man lustful but, at the same time, unable to have sex
31-2 **In conclusion … leaves him:** so drink deceives the drinker
34-5 **requited him:** paid him back (drink, which he is talking of as an equivocator)
36-7 **though he took … cast him:** though he made me fall, I managed to get rid of him, by being sick (using the vocabulary of a wrestling match)

43

Macbeth (without trousers) and Macduff, 2001 production.

1 At this point in the play, why does Macbeth appear on stage without his trousers?

2 What point in the scene is this? Give reasons for your answer. (It is on page 45.)

Jasper Britton and Liam Brennan

(It is on page 45.)

Director's view

Bill Buckhurst
Director, spring 2010

And what is lovely about it is that we, as the audience, know the truth that no one else on stage does, and we're interested to see how Macbeth deals with the arrival of these people – how cool he is. It all depends on how the actor plays it, but the words Macbeth has been given are very, very good and can be very amusing for an audience. Once Macduff's gone off to look for Duncan, Lennox talks about these strange things that have happened that night, almost like omens. And Macbeth just listens and he responds in a half line: "'Twas a rough night". It always brings the house down – I've never seen it in this show with the audience not finding it hilarious! Talk about the understatement of the century!

So the scene then builds, as all these people arrive on stage, discovering the news of the killing. Macbeth obviously goes to the extremes by going off and killing the two grooms. He is questioned by Macduff: "Why did you do it"? And Macbeth starts talking, digging himself a grave, about why he did it. So much so, that it builds to Lady Macbeth (who we think, in rehearsals, is actually faking the faint, to distract attention away for him) and it's very exciting.

SHAKESPEARE'S WORLD

Weather portents

People in Shakespeare's time had a collection of rhymes and phrases to predict the weather, just as we do today. They might look at the sky, rivers or at the behaviour of animals and forecast snow, sunshine or storms. Their sayings, like ours, were based on experience and evidence, as well as folklore.

Superstitious members of the Globe audience made predictions about their own lives based on the weather. Some thought thunder on Monday meant a woman would die, while thunder on Thursday promised plenty of sheep. Some thought the weather's direction showed its nature; an east wind, for example, was thought to be evil, as explained in the Bible. Earthquakes, as mentioned by Lennox in *Macbeth*, were seen as a sign of God's anger, sent to make sinners repent.

Enter Macbeth not seen at first by Macduff.

Macduff Is thy master stirring?
Our knocking has awak'd him. Here he comes.

Lennox Good morrow, noble sir.

Macbeth Good morrow, both! 40

Macduff Is the king stirring, worthy thane?

Macbeth Not yet.

Macduff He did command me to call timely on him,
I have almost slipped the hour.

Macbeth I'll bring you to him.

Macduff I know this is a joyful trouble to you, 45
But yet 'tis one.

Macbeth The labour we delight in physics pain.
This is the door.

Macduff I'll make so bold to call,
For 'tis my limited service. *Exit Macduff.*

Lennox Goes the king hence today? 50

Macbeth He does. He did appoint so.

Lennox The night has been unruly.
Where we lay, our chimneys were blown down,
And (as they say) lamentings heard i' th' air,
Strange screams of death, 55
And prophesying, with accents terrible,
Of dire combustion and confused events,
New hatched to th' woeful time.
The obscure bird clamoured the live-long night.
Some say the earth was feverous and did shake. 60

Macbeth 'Twas a rough night.

Lennox My young remembrance cannot parallel
A fellow to it. *Enter Macduff.*

Macduff O horror, horror, horror!
Tongue nor heart cannot conceive nor name thee. 65

Macbeth and Lennox What's the matter?

Macduff Confusion now hath made his masterpiece.
Most sacrilegious murder hath broke ope
The Lord's anointed temple, and stole thence
The life o' th' building. 70

Macbeth What is't you say? The life?

Lennox Mean you his majesty?

Macduff Approach the chamber, and destroy your sight
With a new Gorgon. Do not bid me speak.

---

38 **stirring:** awake yet

42 **timely:** early
43 **slipped:** missed

45-6 **this is a ... 'tis one:** you have had pleasure in the king's visit, but it is a lot of work
47 **The labour ... physics pain:** the delight we get from work we enjoy cures any pain it causes
49 **my limited service:** it is part of my job

50 **hence:** away from here

52 **unruly:** wild, stormy

56-8 **prophesying, with accents ... woeful time:** saying, in a horrible tone of voice, that something terrible (bringing confusion, chaos and misery) was about to happen
59 **obscure bird:** owl
59 **clamoured:** hooted loudly

62-3 **My young ... fellow to it:** I can't remember a night this bad but then I'm young

65 **conceive:** think of, imagine
67 **Confusion:** Chaos
67 **masterpiece:** his most important piece of work

68 **sacrilegious:** sin against God
68 **ope:** open
69-70 **The Lord's anointed ... th' building:** the king's body (he was seen as appointed by God) and taken his life

74 **Gorgon:** in Greek myths, a monster who turned those who looked at her to stone

Malcolm and Donalbain kneel over the body of Duncan, summer 2010. Banquo and Macbeth are at the front of the watching group.

1 What has the director done here that goes beyond the text and the stage directions?

2 Why might she have made this decision?

l James McArdle, *r* Craig Vye

FROM THE REHEARSAL ROOM...

LISTENING FOR THE KEY WORDS

In groups of six, read through the *Working Cut*, each taking one part.

- This is a listening activity. Don't look at your script until you need to say your lines. To help you, the person reading will say the next speaker's name. So Don(albain) when you say *What is amiss?* you then say, 'Macbeth'.

- Each time before you say your own lines, you must repeat the most important word or phrase that the character before you has just said. Listen hard, and don't cheat by reading.

1 a) What did you notice about the important words or phrases that were chosen?

b) Were there any patterns in the words or any particular types of words that were repeated?

2 Does looking at the important words chosen for each character help us understand more about the characters and their relationships in this scene? Explain your answer.

Working Cut – text for experiment

Mac	Had I but died an hour before this chance,
	I had lived a blessed time. For from this instant
	There's nothing serious in mortality.
Don	What is amiss?
Mac	You are, and do not know't.
Duff	Your royal father's murdered.
Malc	O, by whom?
Len	Those of his chamber, as it seemed, had done't.
	Their hands and faces were all badged with blood.
Mac	O, yet I do repent me of my fury,
	That I did kill them.
Malc	Why do we hold our tongues?
Don	What should be spoken here?
Banq	Let us meet
	And question this most bloody piece of work
	To know it further.
Mac	Let's briefly put on manly readiness,
	And meet i' th' hall together.
Malc	What will you do? I'll to England.
Don	To Ireland, I.

See, and then speak yourselves.

Exit Macbeth and Lennox.

Awake, awake!   75
Ring the alarum bell. Murder and treason!
Banquo and Donalbain! Malcolm awake!
Shake off this downy sleep, death's counterfeit,
And look on death itself. Up, up, and see
The great doom's image. Malcolm, Banquo,   80
As from your graves rise up, and walk like sprites
To countenance this horror. – Ring the bell!

Bell rings. Enter Lady Macbeth.

Lady Macbeth   What's the business?
That such a hideous trumpet calls to parley
The sleepers of the house? Speak, speak!   85

Macduff   O gentle lady,
'Tis not for you to hear what I can speak.
The repetition, in a woman's ear,
Would murder as it fell.

Enter Banquo.

O Banquo, Banquo! Our royal master's murdered.   90

Lady Macbeth   Woe, alas!
What, in our house?

Banquo   Too cruel anywhere.
Dear Duff, I pr'ythee, contradict thyself,
And say it is not so.

Enter Macbeth, Lennox and Ross.

Macbeth   Had I but died an hour before this chance,   95
I had lived a blessed time. For from this instant
There's nothing serious in mortality.
All is but toys. Renown and grace is dead,
The wine of life is drawn, and the mere lees
Is left this vault to brag of.   100

Enter Malcolm and Donalbain.

Donalbain   What is amiss?

Macbeth   You are, and do not know't.
The spring, the head, the fountain of your blood
Is stopped, the very source of it is stopped.

Macduff   Your royal father's murdered.

Malcolm   O, by whom?

Lennox   Those of his chamber, as it seemed, had done't.   105
Their hands and faces were all badged with blood,
So were their daggers, which, unwiped, we found
Upon their pillows. They stared and were distracted.
No man's life was to be trusted with them.

Macbeth   O, yet I do repent me of my fury,   110

---

78 **downy:** soft, cosy

80 **The great doom's image:** a sight as horrifying as the Last Judgement (when the dead rise to be judged by Christ)
81 **sprites:** spirits
82 **countenance:** look on

84 **That such ... parley:** that you call everyone to you so loudly

88-9 **The repetition ... as it fell:** telling a woman this news would kill her

93 **pr'ythee:** short for 'I pray you', please

95 **chance:** event

97-8 **serious in mortality ... toys:** life and death are unimportant, everything's trivial
98 **Renown and grace:** honour
99-100 **The wine ... brag of:** The wine of life's been taken from the barrel, the cellar's empty, there's nothing left to boast of but the bitter sediment at the bottom
101 **What is amiss?:** What's wrong?
102 **The spring ... your blood:** your father
103 **stopped:** dead

106 **badged:** marked

108 **distracted:** confused, befuddled

Laura Rogers
Lady Macbeth, summer 2010

In our version we decided that it was a real faint, because the Lady Macbeth I was trying to portray was one that didn't ever think about the future. Everything was in the moment. The only way she thinks that they can become king and queen is by getting rid of Duncan, but she hasn't thought about anything after that. So, she doesn't realise how it will affect her later. She thinks that if they're king and queen, that's it. Their lives are complete, happiness forever, power, everything. In our version Macbeth carried Duncan out, so it's not just seeing that, but also seeing the grooms being dragged on and the realisation that they're in a very sticky situation and so, in our production, it was a real faint, it was just everything. The fact that they built up to this and suddenly it all became too much. We did speak about the idea that it's a distraction because things are getting a bit heated but we abandoned that idea.

Claire Cox
Lady Macbeth, spring 2010

I think the fainting [is] an acting choice because I think they've been through a hell of a thing. He's killed Duncan, it's happened, so at this point she's very excited. So, once Duncan's body is discovered, murdered in the house, she has to put on a hell of an act. I think when Macbeth comes down having killed the grooms' men, it could be possible that the situation in front of all these people makes her so tense that she hyperventilates, so on one level the faint could be real.

[But] the preference that I had was that it was pretend – an act in front of everyone. He is ranting and raving, and he's starting to get fired up, that might be a bit of a concern for her so another thing she could be doing is trying to shut him up. So, if she faints, if everyone is worried about her, people will stop listening to him.

Members of the Court including Banquo (partly obscured), Malcolm (back to us) and Macbeth (white shirt), spring 2010.

1 Which line was being spoken when this photo was taken? Quote to support your answer.

2 What have the director and the actor playing Macbeth done to show his state of mind?

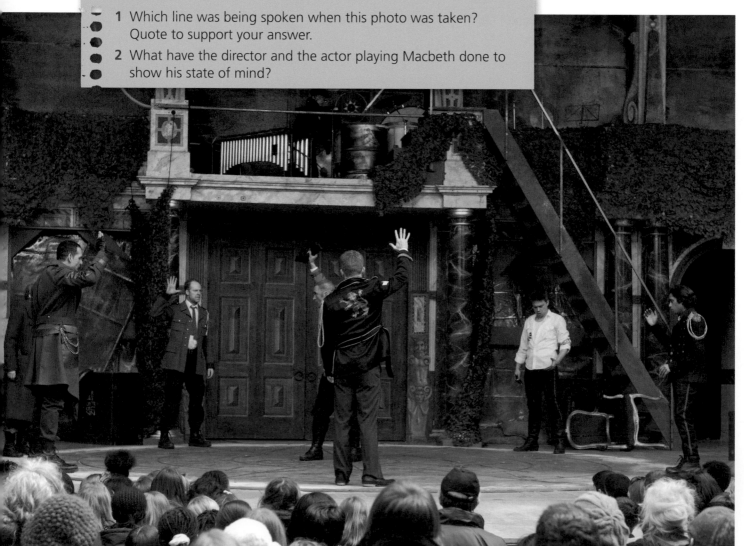

	That I did kill them.
Macduff	Wherefore did you so?
Macbeth	Who can be wise, amazed, temperate, and furious,
	Loyal, and neutral, in a moment? No man.
	Th' expedition of my violent love
	Outran the pauser, reason. Here lay Duncan,
	His silver skin laced with his golden blood,
	And his gashed stabs looked like a breach in nature
	For ruin's wasteful entrance. There the murderers,
	Steeped in the colours of their trade, their daggers
	Unmannerly breeched with gore. Who could refrain,
	That had a heart to love, and in that heart
	Courage to make's love known?
Lady Macbeth	Help me hence, ho!
Macduff	Look to the Lady.

[Lady Macbeth faints, or pretends to faint. While others look after her, Malcolm and Donalbain talk.]

Malcolm	Why do we hold our tongues,
	That most may claim this argument for ours?
Donalbain	What should be spoken here,
	Where our fate hid in an auger hole,
	May rush, and seize us? Let's away,
	Our tears are not yet brewed.
Malcolm	Nor our strong sorrow upon the foot of motion.
Banquo	Look to the Lady.

[Lady Macbeth may be helped offstage.]

	And when we have our naked frailties hid,
	That suffer in exposure, let us meet
	And question this most bloody piece of work
	To know it further. Fears and scruples shake us.
	In the great hand of God I stand, and thence,
	Against the undivulged pretence, I fight
	Of treasonous malice.
Macduff	And so do I.
All	So all.
Macbeth	Let's briefly put on manly readiness,
	And meet i' th' hall together.
All	Well contented.

Exit all except Malcolm and Donalbain.

Malcolm	What will you do? Let's not consort with them.
	To show an unfelt sorrow is an office
	Which the false man does easy. I'll to England.
Donalbain	To Ireland, I. Our separated fortune
	Shall keep us both the safer. Where we are,
	There's daggers in men's smiles. The near in blood,
	The nearer bloody.

---

111 **Wherefore:** why

112 **temperate:** calm

114–5 **Th' expedition ... pauser, reason:** my love for Duncan was so great I acted without thinking
116 **laced with:** covered in streaks of
117–8 **breach in nature ... wasteful entrance:** the castle walls were broken down to let the enemy in (describing the wounds that caused Duncan's death)
119 **Steeped in ... their trade:** soaked in blood
120 **Unmannerly breeched with gore:** indecently covered in blood
122 **make's:** make his

125 **That most ... argument for ours:** letting others show the grief we have most right to (as his sons)
126–8 **What should ... seize us:** What can we say when we don't know who the murderer is and we may be next?
130 **upon the foot of motion:** ready to flow
132–3 **our naked ... in exposure:** dressed

135 **scruples:** doubts, suspicions
136–8 **In the great hand ... malice:** I trust God to protect me and help me fight these unknown traitors

140 **briefly put on manly readiness:** take a moment to quickly dress

143 **consort:** meet with
143 **office:** action
146–7 **Our separate ... the safer:** We'll be safer apart
148–9 **The near in ... nearer bloody:** As Duncan's sons we are most in danger of getting killed next

Malcolm	This murderous shaft that's shot	150
	Hath not yet lighted, and our safest way	
	Is to avoid the aim. Therefore to horse,	
	And let us not be dainty of leave-taking,	
	But shift away. There's warrant in that theft	
	Which steals itself, when there's no mercy left.	155

Exit Malcolm and Donalbain.

ACT 2 SCENE 4

Enter Ross, with an old man.

Old Man	Threescore and ten I can remember well:	
	Within the volume of which time I have seen	
	Hours dreadful and things strange. But this sore night	
	Hath trifled former knowings.	
Ross	Ha, good father,	5
	Thou seest, the heavens, as troubled with man's act,	
	Threaten his bloody stage. By th' clock 'tis day,	
	And yet dark night strangles the travelling lamp.	
	Is't night's predominance, or the day's shame,	
	That darkness does the face of earth entomb,	10
	When living light should kiss it?	
Old Man	'Tis unnatural,	
	Even like the deed that's done. On Tuesday last,	
	A falcon, towering in her pride of place,	
	Was by a mousing owl hawked at and killed.	15
Ross	And Duncan's horses, (a thing most strange and certain)	
	Beauteous and swift, the minions of their race,	
	Turned wild in nature, broke their stalls, flung out,	
	Contending 'gainst obedience, as they would	
	Make war with mankind.	20
Old Man	'Tis said they ate each other.	
Ross	They did so, to th' amazement of mine eyes	
	That looked upon't.	

Enter Macduff.

	Here comes the good Macduff.	
	How goes the world, sir, now?	
Macduff	Why, see you not?	
Ross	Is't known who did this more than bloody deed?	25
Macduff	Those that Macbeth hath slain.	
Ross	Alas, the day!	
	What good could they pretend?	
Macduff	They were suborned.	
	Malcolm and Donalbain, the king's two sons,	
	Are stol'n away and fled, which puts upon them	
	Suspicion of the deed.	

150–2 This murderous … avoid the aim: Let's leave, before we become the targets

153 dainty of leave-taking: concerned to say goodbye properly

154–5 There's warrant … no mercy left: stealing away is justified under the circumstances

Director's Note, 2.3

✔ A drunken Porter lets in Macduff and Lennox to wake up Duncan.

✔ Macbeth joins them, while Macduff goes to wake Duncan.

✔ Macduff returns with the news Duncan is dead.

✔ Macbeth and Lennox go to see. When they return Lennox says the guards did it, and Macbeth says he killed them.

✔ Why do Duncan's sons decide to flee abroad?

1 Threescore and ten: seventy years

2 volume: space

3 sore: bitter, painful

4 Hath trifled former knowings: they are nothing compared to this

6–7 as troubled … bloody stage: disturbed by what has happened, threaten the earth

8 travelling lamp: the sun

9–11 Is't night's … kiss it?: Is it so dark because night is more powerful, or because the day is too ashamed to show its face?

14 towering in her pride of place: at the highest point of her flight

15 a mousing owl: an owl that usually lives off mice (owls would not normally attack a falcon)

17 minions of their race: most elegant of their kind

19 Contending 'gainst obedience: rebelling against their training

19 as: as if

27 What good could they pretend?: What benefit could they expect to gain by it?

27 suborned: bribed

Ross	'Gainst nature still.	30
	Thriftless ambition, that wilt ravin up	
	Thine own life's means. Then 'tis most like	
	The sovereignty will fall upon Macbeth.	
Macduff	He is already named; and gone to Scone	
	To be invested.	35
Ross	Where is Duncan's body?	
Macduff	Carried to Colmekill,	
	The sacred storehouse of his predecessors,	
	And guardian of their bones.	
Ross	Will you to Scone?	
Macduff	No cousin, I'll to Fife.	40
Ross	Well, I will thither	
Macduff	Well, may you see things well done there. Adieu,	
	Lest our old robes sit easier than our new.	
Ross	Farewell, father.	
Old Man	God's benison go with you, and with those	45
	That would make good of bad, and friends of foes.	

Exit all.

30–2 'Gainst nature ... life's means: Another unnatural act – devouring the body that gave them life
32 like: likely
34 Scone: where Scottish kings were crowned
35 invested: crowned
37 Colmekill: the island where Scottish kings were buried

41 thither: there (to Scone)

43 Lest our old ... our new: It is possible that our new situation will be worse than the old one (using clothing imagery)
45 benison: blessing

ACT 3 SCENE 1

Enter Banquo.

Banquo	Thou hast it now, king, Cawdor, Glamis, all,	
	As the weird women promised, and, I fear,	
	Thou play'dst most foully for't. Yet it was said	
	It should not stand in thy posterity,	
	But that myself should be the root and father	5
	Of many kings. If there come truth from them,	
	As upon thee Macbeth, their speeches shine,	
	Why, by the verities on thee made good,	
	May they not be my oracles as well,	
	And set me up in hope? But hush, no more.	10

3 play'dst most foully for't: acted evilly to get it
4 It should not ... posterity: your sons would not be king
6 them: the Witches
8 verities on thee made good: promises that have come true for you
9 oracles: predictors of the future

FROM THE REHEARSAL ROOM...

FREEZE FRAMES

- Create a *freeze frame* to sum up Banquo's thoughts and feelings in his short soliloquy on this page.
1 Explain which lines and words are the most important in the creation of your picture.
2 What are the differences and similarities between Banquo's attitude here and Macbeth's attitude in his soliloquy on page 27 ('If it were done ...')?

Director's Note, 2.4

✔ Ross and an old man discuss unnatural happenings, which suggest evil times.
✔ Macduff joins them, bringing the news that because Malcolm and Donalbain have fled, they are blamed for Duncan's murder.
✔ Macbeth has been chosen king.
✔ What difference is there in Ross' and Macduff's reaction to the news that Macbeth is the new king?

'Enter Macbeth as King, Lady Macbeth as Queen', spring 2010.

1 What has the director done to show Macbeth's new royal status?

2 Explain, with quotations from page 53, how Shakespeare showed Macbeth's new status.

Claire Cox and James Garnon

FROM THE REHEARSAL ROOM...

SECRETS

Work in pairs, **A** and **B**. Your teacher will give each of you a secret objective for the conversation.

- Improvise a short conversation. In it, each of you tries to achieve your objective, without letting the other person know what it is.

- At the end you should each say what you thought the other's secret instruction was.

1 What tactics did you use in the conversation to get what you wanted?

2 Who was the most successful and why?

- Read the *Working Cut* for this scene.

3 How does this interaction between Macbeth and Banquo compare to the conversation that you both just had?

4 Why does Macbeth need specific information from Banquo and what does he do to get it?

6 Why does Banquo not reveal the information that Macbeth wants and how does he do this?

Working Cut – text for experiment

Mac	Here's our chief guest.
	Tonight we hold a solemn supper, sir,
	And I'll request your presence.
Ban	Let your highness command upon me.
Mac	Ride you this afternoon?
Ban	Ay, my good lord.
Mac	Is't far you ride?
Ban	As far, my lord, as will fill up the time
	'Twixt this and supper
Mac	Fail not our feast.
Banquo	My lord, I will not.
Mac	Hie you to horse.
	Adieu, till you return at night.
	Goes Fleance with you?
Ban	Ay, my good lord. Our time does call upon's.
Mac	I wish your horses swift and sure of foot.
	And so I do commend you to their backs.
	Farewell. *[Exit Banquo.]*
	We will keep ourself till supper time alone.
	While then, God be with you!

A trumpet call is played.
Enter Macbeth as King, Lady Macbeth as Queen,
Lennox, Ross, Lords and Attendants.

Macbeth	Here's our chief guest.
Lady Macbeth	If he had been forgotten, It had been as a gap in our great feast, And all-thing unbecoming.
Macbeth	Tonight we hold a solemn supper, sir, 15 And I'll request your presence.
Banquo	Let your highness Command upon me, to the which my duties Are with a most indissoluble tie For ever knit. 20
Macbeth	Ride you this afternoon?
Banquo	Ay, my good lord.
Macbeth	We should have else desired your good advice (Which still hath been both grave and prosperous) In this day's council. But we'll talk tomorrow. Is't far you ride? 25
Banquo	As far, my lord, as will fill up the time 'Twixt this and supper. Go not my horse the better, I must become a borrower of the night, For a dark hour or twain.
Macbeth	Fail not our feast.
Banquo	My lord, I will not. 30
Macbeth	We hear our bloody cousins are bestowed In England and in Ireland, not confessing Their cruel parricide, filling their hearers With strange invention. But of that tomorrow; When therewithal, we shall have cause of state 35 Craving us jointly. Hie you to horse. Adieu, till you return at night. Goes Fleance with you?
Banquo	Ay, my good lord. Our time does call upon's.
Macbeth	I wish your horses swift and sure of foot. 40 And so I do commend you to their backs. Farewell. *Exit Banquo.* Let every man be master of his time Till seven at night, to make society The sweeter welcome. 45 We will keep ourself till supper time alone. While then, God be with you!
	Exit all but Macbeth and a servant.
	Sirrah, a word with you. Attend those men Our pleasure?
Servant	They are, my lord, without the palace gate. 50

14 **all-thing:** completely

19–20 **with a most … knit:** tied with an unbreakable knot

22 **else:** otherwise

23 **Which still … and prosperous:** Which has always been carefully considered and useful

24 **this day's council:** today's meeting with my advisors

27–9 **Go not my horse … twain:** even now, no matter how fast I ride, it will be dark for an hour or two before I get back

31 **bloody cousins:** Malcolm and Donalbain ('bloody' to remind people that they are said to have killed Duncan)

33 **parricide:** killing of their father

34 **strange invention:** unbelievable lies

35–6 **When therewithal … jointly:** When we will also need to discuss matters of government

39 **Our time does call upon's:** We really must go

43 **be master of his time:** be free to do as he likes

44–5 **society The sweeter welcome:** meeting together again something to look forward to

47 **While:** until

48 **Sirrah:** You, used to call a less important person

48–9 **Attend those men Our pleasure?:** Are the men waiting?

50 **without:** outside

A

FROM THE REHEARSAL ROOM...

WHISPERS

- In pairs, one of you is **A** and one **B**.
- First: **A** reads Macbeth's soliloquy (lines 52–76) to your partner in a normal voice.
- Next, **B** whispers the soliloquy to **A**, as quietly as possible while still being heard.

1 Explain how different it feels when the soliloquy is whispered.
2 What letter sounds become more significant when the soliloquy is whispered?

Macbeth during the soliloquy (lines 52–76)

1 Explain what similarities there are in the staging of the soliloquy in these two productions.

2 Pick a line from the soliloquy which Elliot Cowan was most likely to be speaking when the photo was taken. Quote from the text to support your answer.

James Garnon, spring 2010.

Elliot Cowan, summer 2010.

B

FROM THE REHEARSAL ROOM...

DON'T SAY THE WORD

- Form groups of three, with one **A** and two **B**s in each group.
- A, you must ask the **B**s to do something, without ever actually using any words for what you want them to do.
- **B**s, you must try to understand what **A** wants. You can talk, but you can't ask them what they want you to do.

1 What tactics did **A** use to get the idea across without actually saying what he/she wanted? Did they work?

- Now read Macbeth's talk with the murderers (from line 124 to the end of the scene). **A** reads Macbeth, and the **B**s are 1st and 2nd Murderers.

2 How close does Macbeth get to asking the Murderers to kill Banquo? Quote from the text to support your answer.

3 What tactics does Macbeth use to get the Murderers to kill Banquo without ever using the words?

Macbeth Bring them before us. *Exit Servant.*

To be thus, is nothing, but to be safely thus.
Our fears in Banquo stick deep,
And in his royalty of nature reigns that
Which would be feared. 'Tis much he dares,   55
And, to that dauntless temper of his mind,
He hath a wisdom that doth guide his valour
To act in safety. There is none but he
Whose being I do fear. And under him
My genius is rebuked, as it is said   60
Mark Antony's was by Caesar. He chid the sisters,
When first they put the name of king upon me,
And bade them speak to him. Then prophet-like,
They hailed him father to a line of kings.
Upon my head they placed a fruitless crown,   65
And put a barren sceptre in my grip,
Thence to be wrenched with an unlineal hand,
No son of mine succeeding. If't be so,
For Banquo's issue have I 'filed my mind:
For them, the gracious Duncan have I murdered: 70
Put rancours in the vessel of my peace
Only for them: and mine eternal jewel
Given to the common enemy of man,
To make them kings: the seed of Banquo kings.
Rather than so, come Fate, into the list,   75
And champion me to th' utterance! — Who's there?

Enter Servant, and two Murderers.

Macbeth [To the servant.]
Now go to the door, and stay there till we call.

Exit Servant.

Was it not yesterday we spoke together?

Murderers It was, so please your highness.

Macbeth Well then,   80
Now have you considered of my speeches?
Know that it was he, in the times past,
Which held you so under fortune,
Which you thought had been our innocent self.
This I made good to you in our last conference,   85
Passed in probation with you.
How you were borne in hand, how crossed,
The instruments, who wrought with them,
And all things else that might
To half a soul and to a notion crazed   90
Say, "Thus did Banquo."

1st Murderer You made it known to us.

Macbeth I did so, and went further, which is now
Our point of second meeting. Do you find
Your patience so predominant in your nature,   95
That you can let this go? Are you so gospelled,
To pray for this good man and for his issue,

---

52 **To be ... safely thus:** To be king is nothing unless I keep the crown

53–5 **Our fears in Banquo ... would be feared:** I fear Banquo has a natural nobility that looks king-like

56 **dauntless temper of his mind:** brave nature

60–1 **My genius ... Caesar:** my guiding spirit is held back as Mark Antony's spirit was held back by Octavius Caesar's (in Roman times)

61 **chid the sisters:** told the Witches off

63 **bade:** told

65–6 **fruitless crown ... my grip:** they made me king but not the father of kings

67 **Thence to be wrenched ... unlineal hand:** the crown will be taken from me by someone else's children

69 **'filed:** defiled, polluted

71 **Put rancours ... my peace:** filled my calm mind with bitter thoughts

72 **mine eternal jewel:** my soul

73 **the common enemy of man:** the devil

75 **Rather than so:** rather than have that happen

75 **list:** tournament, contest

76 **champion me to th' utterance!:** I'll fight you to stop that prophesy coming true!

82 **he:** refers to Banquo

83 **Which held you ... under fortune:** Who kept you from the good luck you deserved

85 **made ... conference:** explained last time we talked

86 **Passed in probation:** proved

87–8 **borne in hand ... with them:** deceived and obstructed and how he did this

90–1 **To half a soul ... Banquo":** make Banquo's guilt clear even to a half-wit or a madman

94–6 **Do you find ... gospelled:** Are you going to let him get away with this? Are you so full of Christian charity

55

Macbeth and the Murderers, A: 2001, B: summer 2010

1 Explain how and why the body language is so similar in these two shots.
2 How far does the body language reflect the text of Macbeth's speeches on page 57?

A: *l–r* Richard Attlee, Jasper Britton, Jan Knightley; B: *l–r* Michael Camp, Elliot Cowan, Craig Vye

	Whose heavy hand hath bowed you to the grave,
	And beggared yours forever?
1st Murderer	We are men, my liege. 100
Macbeth	Ay, in the catalogue ye go for men,
	As hounds, and greyhounds, mongrels, spaniels, curs,
	Shoughs, water-rugs, and demi-wolves are clept
	All by the name of dogs. The valued file
	Distinguishes the swift, the slow, the subtle, 105
	The house-keeper, the hunter, every one
	According to the gift which bounteous nature
	Hath in him closed, whereby he does receive
	Particular addition, from the bill
	That writes them all alike. And so of men. 110
	Now, if you have a station in the file,
	Not i' th' worst rank of manhood, say 't,
	And I will put that business in your bosoms
	Whose execution takes your enemy off,
	Grapples you to the heart and love of us, 115
	Who wear our health but sickly in his life,
	Which in his death were perfect.
2nd Murderer	I am one, my liege,
	Whom the vile blows and buffets of the world
	Have so incensed that I am reckless what 120
	I do to spite the world.
1st Murderer	And I another,
	So weary with disasters, tugged with fortune,
	That I would set my life on any chance,
	To mend it or be rid on't.
Macbeth	Both of you
	Know Banquo was your enemy. 125
Murderers	True, my lord.
Macbeth	So is he mine, and in such bloody distance
	That every minute of his being thrusts
	Against my near'st of life. And though I could
	With barefaced power sweep him from my sight, 130
	And bid my will avouch it, yet I must not,
	For certain friends that are both his and mine,
	Whose loves I may not drop, but wail his fall
	Who I myself struck down. And thence it is
	That I to your assistance do make love; 135
	Masking the business from the common eye
	For sundry weighty reasons.
2nd Murderer	We shall, my lord,
	Perform what you command us.
1st Murderer	Though our lives—
Macbeth	Your spirits shine through you. Within this hour at most
	I will advise you where to plant yourselves, 141
	Acquaint you with the perfect spy o' th' time,
	The moment on't, for't must be done tonight,

98 **heavy hand ... to the grave:** ill-treatment has almost killed you
99 **beggared yours:** left your family poor
101 **catalogue:** list of living things
103 **clept:** called
104 **valued file:** the list that sorts them by their qualities
106 **house-keeper:** watchdog
108 **Hath in him closed:** has given him
109–10 **Particular addition... all alike:** the qualities that make him stand out from the rest
111 **station in the file:** place in the list
112 **worst rank:** lowest level
113–5 **put that business ... love of us:** outline a plan so you can kill your enemy and earn my favour
116–7 **Who wear ... perfect:** For I will never be comfortable while he lives
119 **blows and buffets:** punches, awful setbacks
120 **incensed that I am reckless:** angry that I don't care
122 **tugged with fortune:** tossed about by fate
123 **set my life ... chance:** take any gamble with my life
124 **To mend ... on't:** to improve it or die
127 **bloody distance:** dangerous hostility (refers to space between fencers sword-fighting)
128–9 **thrusts ... of life:** stabs my heart
130 **With barefaced ... sight:** have him executed, because I am king
133 **loves I may not drop:** support I can't afford to lose
133–4 **but wail ... struck down:** I'm arranging his death, but must seem upset by it
135 **to your ... love:** ask you to help me
136 **Masking ... common eye:** keeping it secret
137 **sundry weighty:** various important
140 **Your spirits ... you:** You are clearly reliable
142 **perfect spy o' th' time:** the best time to do it

Lady Macbeth and Macbeth, 2001.

Compare this photo with ones from the same production on page 30. Are there any clues in either the text or the body language of the actors that the balance of power is shifting in their relationship? Give reasons for your answer.

Eve Best and Jasper Britton

Working Cut – text for experiment

Lady M	How now, my lord, why do you keep alone. Things without all remedy Should be without regard. What's done is done.
Mac	We have scorched the snake, not killed it.
Lady M	Come on, Be bright and jovial among your guests tonight.
Mac	So shall I love, and so I pray be you. Let your remembrance apply to Banquo. And make our faces vizards to our hearts, Disguising what they are.
Lady M	You must leave this.
Mac	O, full of scorpions is my mind, dear wife! Thou know'st that Banquo and his Fleance lives.
Lady M	But in them nature's copy's not eterne.
Mac	There's comfort yet, they are assailable, Then be thou jocund. Ere the bat hath flown His cloistered flight, there shall be done A deed of dreadful note.
Lady M	What's to be done?
Mac	Be innocent of the knowledge, dearest chuck, Till thou applaud the deed. — Come, seeling night, Scarf up the tender eye of pitiful day. Thou marvell'st at my words: but hold thee still, Things bad begun make strong themselves by ill. So prithee go with me.

FROM THE REHEARSAL ROOM...

FREEZE FRAMES

- In groups of four, read the *Working Cut* for this scene.

- Create three *freeze frames* that capture the essence of the scene and choose a line from the text to go with each *freeze frame*.

- As a whole group, look at the *freeze frames* and unpick what is going on in each image.

1 What moments in the scene is each group illustrating?

2 What do the *freeze frames* tell us about the relationship between Macbeth and Lady Macbeth?

3 The relationship between Macbeth and Lady Macbeth changes in this scene. Identify the key moments (and lines) at which these changes take place.

	And something from the palace, always thought	
	That I require a clearness. And with him,	145
	To leave no rubs nor botches in the work,	
	Fleance, his son, that keeps him company,	
	Whose absence is no less material to me	
	Than is his father's, must embrace the fate	
	Of that dark hour. Resolve yourselves apart,	150
	I'll come to you anon.	
Murderers	We are resolved, my lord.	
Macbeth	I'll call upon you straight. Abide within.—	
	It is concluded. Banquo, thy soul's flight,	
	If it find heaven, must find it out tonight.	155

Exit Macbeth and the Murderers.

ACT 3 SCENE 2

Enter Lady Macbeth and a Servant.

Lady Macbeth	Is Banquo gone from court?	
Servant	Ay, madam, but returns again tonight.	
Lady Macbeth	Say to the king, I would attend his leisure	
	For a few words.	
Servant	Madam, I will. *Exit Servant.*	5
Lady Macbeth	Naught's had, all's spent,	
	Where our desire is got without content.	
	'Tis safer to be that which we destroy,	
	Than by destruction dwell in doubtful joy.	

Enter Macbeth.

	How now, my lord, why do you keep alone,	10
	Of sorriest fancies your companions making,	
	Using those thoughts which should indeed have died	
	With them they think on? Things without all remedy	
	Should be without regard. What's done is done.	
Macbeth	We have scorched the snake, not killed it.	15
	She'll close, and be herself, whilst our poor malice	
	Remains in danger of her former tooth.	
	But let the frame of things disjoint, both the worlds suffer,	
	Ere we will eat our meal in fear, and sleep	
	In the affliction of these terrible dreams	20
	That shake us nightly. Better be with the dead,	
	Whom we, to gain our peace, have sent to peace,	
	Than on the torture of the mind to lie	
	In restless ecstasy. Duncan is in his grave.	
	After life's fitful fever he sleeps well,	25
	Treason has done his worst: nor steel, nor poison,	
	Malice domestic, foreign levy, nothing	
	Can touch him further.	
Lady Macbeth	Come on,	

144 **something:** some distance
144–5 **always thought ... clearness:** remember, I must not be suspected
146 **leave no rubs ... work:** don't make any mistakes
148 **material:** important
149–50 **embrace the fate ... hour:** die too
150 **Resolve yourselves apart:** Go and talk over your decision
151 **anon:** at once
153 **straight:** without delay
153 **Abide within:** Wait inside

3–4 **I would attend ... words:** I'd like to talk to him, as soon as it is convenient

6 **Naught's had, all's spent:** Nothing's gained, everything's wasted
7 **Where our desire ... content:** when getting what we want doesn't make us happy
8–9 **'Tis safer ... doubtful joy:** Better to be murdered than to be a murderer haunted by fear
11 **sorriest fancies:** the most painful thoughts
12–3 **Using those ... think on?:** thinking about the murder of Duncan
12–3 **Things without ...without regard:** if you can't change things, don't brood on them
15 **scorched:** slashed, wounded
16–7 **She'll close ... former tooth:** She'll heal and be a threat to us again
18 **let the frame ... the worlds:** disrupt the proper order of the universe and both heaven and earth
20 **affliction:** misery
22 **to gain ... sent to peace:** have murdered to get what we want
23–4 **on the torture ... ecstasy:** to lie in a frantic, sleepless, trance
25 **fitful fever:** restless, overheated, activity
27 **Malice domestic:** civil war
27 **foreign levy:** foreign invasion

Macbeth and Lady Macbeth watched by the Witches, summer 2010.

Why might the director have added the Witches to this scene?

l–r Elliott Cowan, Laura Rogers, Karen Anderson, Simone Kirby, Janet Fullerlove

Director's Note, 3.2

✔ Neither Lady Macbeth, nor Macbeth, are content.
✔ The audience know Macbeth has planned the murder of Banquo, but he chooses not to tell Lady Macbeth.
✔ How has Shakespeare shown their relationship changing?

Actor's view

Laura Rogers
Lady Macbeth, summer 2010

Interviewer: *Now, Macbeth makes a point of telling you there's something he is not going to tell you. For your Lady Macbeth, does this mark a change in the relationship?*

Laura Rogers: *Yes, definitely. Because, I think, they had been so close and everything, every decision they had made, they made together – or she had made and he would go along with it. She was the driving force, and she planted all the seeds in his head about what to do next, and suddenly, I think this is the first time, that she realizes that her power, her hold over him, isn't as strong anymore, because they had shared everything – he would not have a thought that she didn't know. Now, he was starting to make*

plans by himself and keep her out of it. So, I think she starts to feel alienated, and like her control is slipping and that's when I think when she starts to feel very vulnerable because without him she is nothing. So, if she feels that he is going away from her, in any sense, then she has nothing left and who knows what will happen next?! I don't suppose she felt very safe herself … are his thoughts … are they murderous thoughts? If so, who does he think he needs to kill? Maybe she is worried for her own life and, her own safety. And just the fact that, at that point, I suppose she feels that she is not as loved as she once was. And she finds herself in a very vulnerable position, which she doesn't know how to claw herself back from. Her manipulation isn't working any more.

	Gentle my lord, sleek o'er your rugged looks, 30
	Be bright and jovial among your guests tonight.

Gentle my lord, sleek o'er your rugged looks, 30
Be bright and jovial among your guests tonight.

Macbeth So shall I love, and so I pray be you.
Let your remembrance apply to Banquo.
Present him eminence, both with eye and tongue:
Unsafe the while, that we must lave 35
Our honours in these flattering streams;
And make our faces vizards to our hearts,
Disguising what they are.

Lady Macbeth   You must leave this.

Macbeth O, full of scorpions is my mind, dear wife!
Thou know'st that Banquo and his Fleance lives. 40

Lady Macbeth But in them nature's copy's not eterne.

Macbeth There's comfort yet, they are assailable,
Then be thou jocund. Ere the bat hath flown
His cloistered flight, ere to black Hecate's summons
The shard-borne beetle with his drowsy hums 45
Hath rung night's yawning peal, there shall be done
A deed of dreadful note.

Lady Macbeth   What's to be done?

Macbeth Be innocent of the knowledge, dearest chuck,
Till thou applaud the deed. — Come, seeling night,
Scarf up the tender eye of pitiful day; 50
And with thy bloody and invisible hand
Cancel and tear to pieces that great bond
Which keeps me pale. Light thickens,
And the crow makes wing to th' rooky wood.
Good things of day begin to droop and drowse, 55
Whiles night's black agents to their preys do rouse.
Thou marvell'st at my words: but hold thee still,
Things bad begun make strong themselves by ill.
So prithee go with me.

Exit Macbeth and Lady Macbeth.

ACT 3 SCENE 3

Enter three Murderers.

1st Murderer But who did bid thee join with us?

3rd Murderer   Macbeth.

2nd Murderer He needs not our mistrust, since he delivers
Our offices, and what we have to do,
To the direction just.

1st Muderer   Then stand with us.
The west yet glimmers with some streaks of day. 5
Now spurs the lated traveller apace
To gain the timely inn, and near approaches
The subject of our watch.

3rd Murderer Hark, I hear horses.

30 **sleek o'er:** smooth over
30 **rugged:** troubled, disturbed

33-4 **Let you remembrance ... eminence:** Remember to pay special attention to Banquo
35-6 **Unsafe the while ... streams:** We're not yet secure in our power and must use flattery to keep people on our side
37 **vizards:** masks

41 **in them nature's ... eterne:** they're human, they can't live forever
42 **assailable:** open to attack
43 **jocund:** cheerful
44 **cloistered:** restricted, habitual
44 **Hecate:** goddess of the moon and witchcraft
45-6 **shard-borne beetle ... peal:** dung beetle had brought the night (from an Ancient Egyptian myth)

49 **seeling:** blinding
50 **Scarf up:** blindfold
50 **pitiful:** sympathetic, compassionate
52-3 **Cancel and tear ... pale:** destroy Banquo and Fleance who threaten me (as in tearing up a legal document)
53 **Light thickens:** It's getting darker
56 **night's black agents... rouse:** evil things start hunting
57 **hold thee still:** wait and see
58 **Things bad begun ... ill:** evil deeds have to be followed by more evil deeds

2-3 **He needs not our mistrust ... offices:** We can trust him, he knows our orders
4 **To the direction just:** exactly
5 **yet:** still, even now
6-7 **spurs the lated ... inn:** travellers still on the road hurry to reach the inn before dark
8 **The subject of our watch:** those we're waiting for (Banquo and Fleance)

Third Murderer, Banquo and the first two Murderers, 2001

l–r Patrick Brennan, Richard Attlee, Jan Knightley

A Murderer and Banquo, spring 2010.

These photos are from different productions. Work out which line or stage direction each one goes with. Quote from the text to support your answer.

l–r Philip Cumbus, Matt Costain

Director's Note, 3.3

✔ The Murderers lie in wait for Banquo and Fleance.
✔ They attack in the dark, but Fleance escapes.
✔ What does Shakespeare do to show Macbeth's growing distrust of everybody?

Banquo	*Within* Give us a light there, ho.	10

| **2nd Murderer** | Then 'tis he. The rest
That are within the note of expectation
Already are i' th' court. |

12 within expectation: invited to the banquet

| **1st Murderer** | His horses go about. |

14 go about: are being led to the stables

| **3rd Murderer** | Almost a mile: but he does usually,
So all men do, from hence to th' palace gate
Make it their walk. | 15 |

Enter Fleance with a torch, and Banquo.

| **2nd Murderer** | A light, a light! |

| **3rd Murderer** | 'Tis he. |

| **1st Murderer** | Stand to 't. | 20 |

20 Stand to 't: Get ready

| **Banquo** | It will be rain tonight. |

| **1st Murderer** | Let it come down. |

22 Let it come down: referring to the rain and the attack

[The murderers attack. The torch goes out.]

| **Banquo** | O, treachery!
Fly good Fleance, fly, fly, fly!
Thou mayst revenge. — O slave! | 25 |

25 Thou mayst … slave: Live to revenge my murder (to Fleance). You villain (to the Murderer)

[Banquo is killed. Fleance escapes.]

| **3rd Murderer** | Who did strike out the light? |

| **1st Murderer** | Was't not the way? |

26 Was't not the way?: Wasn't that the plan?

| **3rd Murderer** | There's but one down. The son is fled. |

| **2nd Murderer** | We have lost best half of our affair. |

28 lost best … affair: let the most important victim escape

| **3rd Murderer** | Well, let's away, and say how much is done. |

Exit the three Murderers.

ACT 3 SCENE 4

A banquet is set out.
Enter Macbeth, Lady Macbeth, Ross, Lennox, other Lords,
and attendants.

| **Macbeth** | You know your own degrees, sit down.
At first and last the hearty welcome. |

1 degrees: social importance (this affected where you could sit)
2 At first and last the: to everyone a

| **Lords** | Thanks to your majesty. |

| **Macbeth** | Ourself will mingle with society,
And play the humble host.
Our hostess keeps her state, but in best time
We will require her welcome. | 5 |

4 society: everyone here

6–7 keeps … welcome: will sit in her place at the table until the right time to welcome you

| **Lady Macbeth** | Pronounce it for me, sir, to all our friends,
For my heart speaks, they are welcome. |

8 Pronounce it for me: Say it for me

Enter first Murderer, inconspicuously.

| **Macbeth** | See, they encounter thee with their hearts' thanks. | 10 |

10 encounter thee: respond

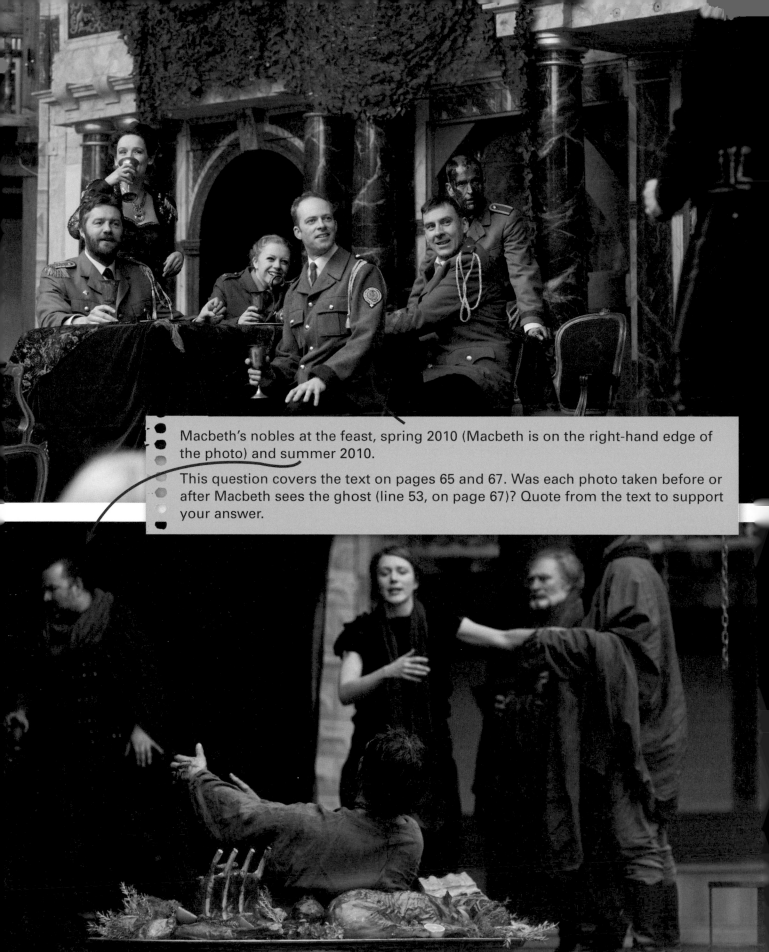

Macbeth's nobles at the feast, spring 2010 (Macbeth is on the right-hand edge of the photo) and summer 2010.

This question covers the text on pages 65 and 67. Was each photo taken before or after Macbeth sees the ghost (line 53, on page 67)? Quote from the text to support your answer.

	Both sides are even. Here I'll sit i' th' midst. Be large in mirth, anon we'll drink a measure The table round. *[To the Murderer.]* There's blood upon thy face.
1st Murderer	'Tis Banquo's then.
Macbeth	'Tis better thee without than he within. 15 Is he despatched?
1st Murderer	My lord, his throat is cut, that I did for him.
Macbeth	Thou art the best o' th' cut-throats, Yet he's good that did the like for Fleance. If thou didst it, thou art the nonpareil. 20
1st Murderer	Most royal sir, Fleance is 'scaped.
Macbeth	Then comes my fit again. I had else been perfect; Whole as the marble, founded as the rock; As broad and general as the casing air. But now I am cabined, cribbed, confined, bound in 25 To saucy doubts and fears. — But Banquo's safe?
1st Murderer	Ay, my good lord. Safe in a ditch he bides, With twenty trenchèd gashes on his head, The least a death to nature.
Macbeth	Thanks for that. — There the grown serpent lies, the worm that's fled 30 Hath nature that in time will venom breed, No teeth for th' present. — Get thee gone, tomorrow We'll hear ourselves again. *Exit Murderer.*
Lady Macbeth	My royal lord, You do not give the cheer. The feast is sold That is not often vouched while 'tis a-making. 35 'Tis given with welcome. To feed were best at home: From thence, the sauce to meat is ceremony, Meeting were bare without it.
	Enter the Ghost of Banquo. He sits in Macbeth's place and is invisible to Lady Macbeth and the Lords.
Macbeth	Sweet remembrancer! Now, good digestion wait on appetite, 40 And health on both!
Lennox	May't please your highness sit.
Macbeth	Here had we now our country's honour, roofed, Were the gracèd person of our Banquo present. Who may I rather challenge for unkindness Than pity for mischance.
Ross	His absence, sir, 45 Lays blame upon his promise. Please't your highness To grace us with your royal company?
Macbeth	The table's full.

11 **Both sides are even:** There are the same number of people on each side of the table
12 **Be large in mirth:** enjoy yourselves
12 **measure ... round:** all drink a toast
15 **'Tis better ... within:** better on you than still inside him
16 **despatched:** killed

20 **the nonpareil:** unequalled

21 **is 'scaped:** has escaped

22 **my fit:** my fears and doubts
24 **perfect:** completely satisfied
23-4 **Whole as ... air:** solid as marble, stable as rock and free as air
25-6 **cabined, cribbed ... saucy:** imprisoned by my uncontrollable
26 **safe:** definitely dead
27 **bides:** will stay
28 **trenchèd:** cut deep (like a trench)
29 **The least ... nature:** the smallest of which would have killed him
30 **grown serpent:** Banquo
30 **worm:** young snake (referring to Fleance)
31-2 **Hath nature ... present:** will be trouble later, but is harmless for now
33 **hear ourselves:** talk
34 **give the cheer:** act like a good host
34-8 **The feast ... without it:** people will feel they are eating out for payment, not with friends. Unless you make them feel at home, they might as well have stayed at home

39 **Sweet remembrancer:** Thank you for reminding me, sweetheart

42 **country's honour:** most important lords in Scotland
42 **roofed:** under the same roof
43 **graced:** worthy, gifted
44-5 **Who may I ... mischance:** who I hope is just rudely late, then I can tell him off, not come to harm
45-6 **His ... promise:** He shouldn't have promised to come if he thought he might not be able to get here

POINTING ON PRONOUNS

- In groups of five read the *Working Cut* of Act 3 Scene 4.

- Decide who will read each part. They are: Macbeth, Lady Macbeth, Lords, Ross and Lennox.

- Set up five chairs as if they are around a table. Everyone should sit on a chair, except the person reading Macbeth.

- Read through the scene and each time your character says a pronoun or proper name point at who or what you are talking to or about (e.g. my, your, our...).

  - Make sure that you really do point at a definite person or place.

  - If your character refers to somebody outside of the group of characters, point away from the imaginary table.

  - If you character refers to Banquo, point at the empty chair.

1 Are there any patterns in the pointing?

2 What does this scene tell us about Macbeth's state of mind?

3 a) How does Lady Macbeth respond to this?

  b) Why does she do this?

4 What might the Lords Ross and Lennox be thinking?

Working Cut – text for experiment

Lady M   My royal lord.
Enter the Ghost of Banquo. He sits in Macbeth's place and is invisible to Lady Macbeth and the Lords.

Mac	Sweet remembrancer!
Len	May't please your highness sit.
Mac	Here had we now our country's honour, roofed,
	Were the graced person of our Banquo present.
Ross	His absence, sir,
	Lays blame upon his promise. Please't your highness
	To grace us with your royal company?
Mac	The table's full.
Len	Here is a place reserved, sir.
Mac	Where?
Len	Here, my good lord.

Macbeth sees the Ghost of Banquo.
           What is't that moves your highness?

Mac	Which of you have done this?
Len	What, my good lord?
Mac	Thou canst not say I did it. Never shake
	Thy gory locks at me.
Ross	Gentlemen, rise, his highness is not well.
Lady M	Sit worthy friends. My lord is often thus,
	And hath been from his youth. Pray you keep seat.
	Are you a man?
Mac	Ay, and a bold one, that dare look on that
	Which might appal the devil.
Lady M	O proper stuff!
	This is the very painting of your fear.
	This is the air-drawn dagger which you said
	Led you to Duncan. When all's done,
	You look but on a stool.
Mac	Prithee see there! *Exit Ghost of Banquo.*
Lady M	What, quite unmanned in folly?
Mac	If I stand here, I saw him.
Lady M	Fie, for shame!
Mac	The time has been,
	That when the brains were out, the man would die,
	And there an end. But now they rise again.
Lady M	My worthy lord,
	Your noble friends do lack you.
Mac	I do forget.
	Do not muse at me my most worthy friends,
	I have a strange infirmity, which is nothing
	To those that know me. *Enter Ghost of Banquo.*
	I drink to th' general joy o' th' whole table,
	And to our dear friend Banquo, whom we miss.
Lords	Our duties, and the pledge.
Mac	*He sees the Ghost of Banquo.*
	Avaunt, and quit my sight!
Lady M	Think of this, good peers,
	But as a thing of custom. 'Tis no other,
Mac	What man dare, I dare.
	Exit Ghost of Banquo. Why, so, being gone,
	I am a man again. – Pray you, sit still.
Lady M	You have displaced the mirth,
	Broke the good meeting, with most admired disorder.
Mac	Can such things be?
	When now I think you can behold such sights,
	And keep the natural ruby of your cheeks,
	When mine is blanched with fear.
Ross	What sights, my lord?
Lady M	I pray you speak not. He grows worse and worse.
	Go at once.
Len	Good night, and better health attend his majesty.
Lady M	A kind good night to all.

Lennox	Here is a place reserved, sir.	
Macbeth	Where?	50
Lennox	Here, my good lord.	

[Macbeth sees the Ghost of Banquo.]

	What is't that moves your highness?	
Macbeth	Which of you have done this?	
Lennox	What, my good lord?	
Macbeth	Thou canst not say I did it. Never shake Thy gory locks at me.	55
Ross	Gentlemen, rise, his highness is not well.	
Lady Macbeth	Sit worthy friends. My lord is often thus, And hath been from his youth. Pray you keep seat, The fit is momentary, upon a thought He will again be well. If much you note him You shall offend him, and extend his passion. Feed, and regard him not. —Are you a man?	60
Macbeth	Ay, and a bold one, that dare look on that Which might appal the devil.	
Lady Macbeth	O proper stuff! This is the very painting of your fear. This is the air-drawn dagger which you said Led you to Duncan. O, these flaws, and starts, Impostors to true fear, would well become A woman's story at a winter's fire, Authorized by her grandam. Shame itself, Why do you make such faces? When all's done, You look but on a stool.	65 70
Macbeth	Prithee see there! Behold! Look! Lo! How say you? Why what care I? If thou canst nod, speak too. If charnel houses and our graves must send Those that we bury, back; our monuments Shall be the maws of kites. *[Exit Ghost of Banquo.]*	75
Lady Macbeth	What, quite unmanned in folly?	
Macbeth	If I stand here, I saw him.	
Lady Macbeth	Fie, for shame!	80
Macbeth	Blood hath been shed ere now, i' th' olden time, Ere human statute purged the gentle weal. Ay, and since too, murders have been performed Too terrible for the ear. The time has been, That when the brains were out, the man would die, And there an end. But now they rise again, With twenty mortal murders on their crowns, And push us from our stools. This is more strange Than such a murder is.	85

52 **moves:** upsets

54 **Thou canst not say I did it:** you can't say I murdered you
55 **gory locks:** hair caked in blood

59 **upon a thought:** in a moment
60 **much … him:** you stare at him
61 **extend his passion:** make his fit last longer

65 **proper stuff:** nonsense
66 **the very painting … fear:** something your fear has made you imagine
67 **flaws:** emotional outbursts
67 **starts:** jerks, twitches
69 **Imposters to true fear:** are nothing compared to real fear
70-1 **A woman's story … grandam:** an old wives' tale

73 **Prithee:** for heaven's sake

76 **charnel houses:** places where the bones of the dead were stored
77-8 **monuments … kites:** tombs will be the stomachs of the birds who feed off the dead
79 **What … folly?:** Has your madness made you lose your manly courage?

81 **ere:** before
82 **Ere human statute … weal:** before people made laws to control behaviour

87 **mortal murders … crowns:** fatal head wounds

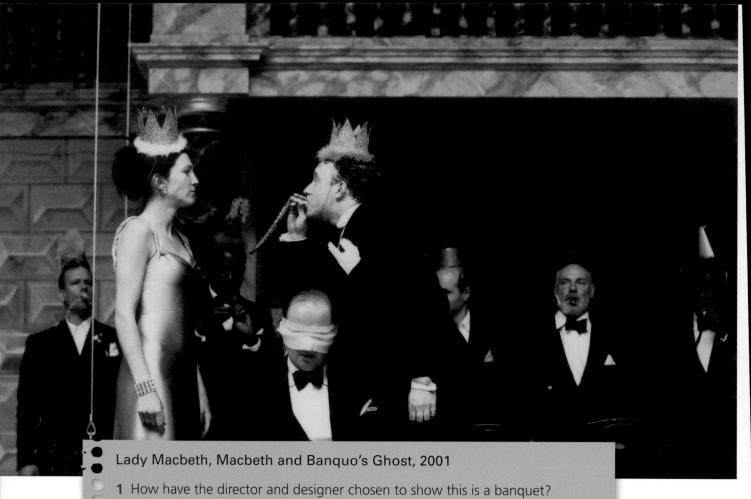

Lady Macbeth, Macbeth and Banquo's Ghost, 2001

1 How have the director and designer chosen to show this is a banquet?

2 Look back at the photos on page 64 as well. You can see three different ways of staging the Ghost. Give a strength and a weakness of each interpretation.

3 What issues do you need to think about when staging the ghost?

Eve Best, Patrick Brennan (blindfolded) and Jasper Britton

Actor's view

James Garnon
Macbeth, spring 2010

I think the only intelligent response is that Macbeth imagines that the Ghost is real; it's real for Macbeth. And I suppose beyond that the only other thing that's interesting about it is that Macbeth imagines that it's real for everyone else, when it obviously isn't. No one else appears to see it, but he appears to see in them that they have, given his reaction to them at the end of the scene. Clearly ghosts are real to Macbeth – that's all we need to know.

In this particular case Banquo's ghost seems to drive him on to a further acceptance of his own nature, a further acceptance of how much he has changed, how much he has moved on; it has driven him to a point where he can contemplate further murders, bizarrely. You think you'd be visited by the ghost and he would then be horrified and cease, but in fact he's horrified, and goes on. Immediately he starts talking about what he's going to do to Macduff.

Actor's view

Julius D'Silva
Ross, summer 2010

We have a large platter, an enormous platter of roasted meats, and fruit and legs of lamb and hams, and you see the platter come onstage with nothing underneath it, rather like the old magic tricks. And then you see a hand, a bloody hand come out of it and grab Macbeth's hand as he leans over the platter of meat, which gets a gasp from the audience. And then gradually you see him pull the ghost of Banquo, as if by magic, out of this platter of bloody meat. And you see Banquo come out from the middle of it, and it's completely unexpected, and it gets a great reaction from the audience.

The hard bit for the actor is of course, not noticing him! Elliot [Cowan, Macbeth] is the only actor who can see Banquo. So we have to follow each others' eye line and we have to be concerned with Macbeth in that moment to try not to stare at this 6 foot 2 man covered in tomato ketchup, who's wandering round the stage.

But it's a great moment and I think one of the most dramatic moments in the whole production really.

Lady Macbeth   My worthy lord,
Your noble friends do lack you.

Macbeth   I do forget.   90
Do not muse at me my most worthy friends,
I have a strange infirmity, which is nothing
To those that know me. Come, love and health to all,
Then I'll sit down. — Give me some wine, fill full. —

Enter Ghost of Banquo.

I drink to th' general joy o' th' whole table,   95
And to our dear friend Banquo, whom we miss.
Would he were here! To all, and him, we thirst,
And all to all.

Lords   Our duties, and the pledge.

Macbeth   *[He sees the Ghost of Banquo.]*
Avaunt, and quit my sight! Let the earth hide thee!
Thy bones are marrowless, thy blood is cold.   100
Thou hast no speculation in those eyes
Which thou dost glare with.

Lady Macbeth   Think of this, good peers,
But as a thing of custom. 'Tis no other,
Only it spoils the pleasure of the time.

Macbeth   What man dare, I dare.   105
Approach thou like the rugged Russian bear,
The armed rhinoceros, or th' Hyrcan tiger,
Take any shape but that, and my firm nerves
Shall never tremble. Or be alive again,
And dare me to the desert with thy sword.   110
If trembling I inhabit then, protest me
The baby of a girl. Hence, horrible shadow!
Unreal mock'ry hence!   *[Exit Ghost of Banquo.]*

Why, so, being gone,
I am a man again. — Pray you, sit still.

Lady Macbeth   You have displaced the mirth,   115
Broke the good meeting, with most admired disorder.

Macbeth   Can such things be,
And overcome us like a summer's cloud,
Without our special wonder? You make me strange
Even to the disposition that I owe,   120
When now I think you can behold such sights,
And keep the natural ruby of your cheeks,
When mine is blanched with fear.

Ross   What sights, my lord?

Lady Macbeth   I pray you speak not. He grows worse and worse.
Question enrages him. At once, good-night.   125
Stand not upon the order of your going,
But go at once.

---

90 **do lack you:** miss your company
91 **muse:** be surprised, wonder
92 **infirmity:** illness

97 **thirst:** drink
98 **And all to all:** and good health to everyone
98 **Our duties, and the pledge:** We confirm our loyalty to you and toast you in return
99 **Avaunt:** Go!

101 **speculation** sight

103 **But as a thing of custom:** as a regular event

106 **rugged:** hairy, shaggy
107 **Hyrcan:** from Hyrcania (south of the Caspian Sea), a wild place famous for tigers
108 **but that:** except Banquo's ghost
110 **to the desert:** to a fight to the death in a lonely place
111-2 **If trembling ... girl:** If I stay trembling indoors then, call me a helpless doll
112 **shadow:** ghost

115 **displaced the mirth:** spoiled everyone's evening
116 **most admired disorder:** disturbing behaviour no one could ignore

119 **Without our special wonder?:** without me noticing and reacting to it
119-23 **You make me ... blanched with fear:** I thought I was brave but this vision has made me white with fear yet you look at it unmoved

126 **Stand ... going:** don't go in order of importance, just go quickly

Lennox	Good night, and better health Attend his majesty.
Lady Macbeth	A kind good night to all.

Exit all but Macbeth and Lady Macbeth.

Macbeth	It will have blood they say. Blood will have blood. Stones have been known to move, and trees to speak. Augurs, and understood relations, have By magot-pies and choughs and rooks brought forth The secret'st man of blood. — What is the night?	130
Lady Macbeth	Almost at odds with morning, which is which.	135
Macbeth	How say'st thou that Macduff denies his person At our great bidding?	
Lady Macbeth	Did you send to him, sir?	
Macbeth	I hear it by the way, but I will send. There's not a one of them but in his house I keep a servant fee'd. I will tomorrow (And betimes I will) to the weird sisters. More shall they speak. For now I am bent to know By the worst means, the worst. For mine own good, All causes shall give way. I am in blood Stepped in so far, that should I wade no more, Returning were as tedious as go o'er. Strange things I have in head, that will to hand, Which must be acted, ere they may be scanned.	140 145
Lady Macbeth	You lack the season of all natures, sleep.	150
Macbeth	Come, we'll to sleep. My strange and self-abuse Is the initiate fear that wants hard use. We are yet but young in deed.	

They exit.

130 **It will have blood... Blood will have blood:** murder will lead to more murder

132 **Augers ... relations:** prophesies and knowing how events are connected

133 **magot-pies ... rooks:** magpies, crows and rooks (birds foretelling bad luck)

133–4 **brought forth ... man of blood:** revealed the most cunning hidden murderers

135 **Almost at odds ... which is which:** somewhere between night and day

136 **How say'st thou:** What do you think of the fact that

136–7 **denies his person ... bidding?:** chose not to come to court, despite my command to do so?

139 **by the way:** from my spies

140 **them:** the nobles

141 **fee'd:** paid (to spy)

142 **betimes:** very early

143 **bent:** determined

144 **by the worst means:** by witchcraft

144 **For mine own good:** to get what I want

146 **should:** even if

148 **in head:** planned

148 **to hand:** be done

149 **acted, ere ... scanned:** carried out before I can think about them too hard

150 **season of all natures:** the thing we need to keep us fresh

151 **self-abuse:** self-deception

152 **initiate:** beginner's

152 **wants hard use:** needs practice

153 **young in deed:** new to murder

Macbeth and Lady Macbeth after the lords have left.

1 Pick a line that could have been spoken when photo B was taken. Give reasons for your answer.

2 Looking at these two photographs, what can you deduce about the different way the two productions interpreted the relationship between Macbeth and Lady Macbeth at this point in the play?

Above, James Garnon and Claire Cox, spring 2010; below, Elliot Cowan and Laura Rogers, summer 2010.

Director's Note, 3.4

✔ As Macbeth entertains his nobles at a banquet, the Murderer reports that Banquo is dead, but Fleance escaped.

✔ He rejoins the banquet, then sees Banquo's Ghost. Nobody else can see it, or understand Macbeth's behaviour.

✔ Lady Macbeth tries to cover up, saying it is an old illness, but, just as he recovers, Macbeth sees the Ghost again.

✔ Again the nobles are worried, and this time Lady Macbeth tells them to leave.

✔ When they are alone, Macbeth decides to visit the Witches for more prophesies.

✔ What effect will these events have on the nobles' view of Macbeth as King?

EXAMINER'S NOTES, 3.4

These questions help you to explore many aspects of *Macbeth*. At GCSE, your teacher will tell you which aspects are relevant to how your Shakespeare response will be assessed.

EXAMINER'S TIP

A good response

A good response may include more than one way of interpreting a scene. The key word is 'or'. For example, in this scene Macbeth can be seen as losing control. He speaks to Banquo's ghost in a way that may let people know he has murdered him. Or, you could think he is becoming more in control because, despite this event, he is making plans for his next moves, and without help from Lady Macbeth.

You might add thoughts about Shakespeare's purpose as a dramatist – to keep the audience undecided, because both interpretations are possible and we need to keep watching to make up our minds.

① Character and plot development

So far, Macbeth has been presented as a ruthless, brave and loyal soldier, a man with a conscience and ambition, whose life is changed by a supernatural encounter. Here we see him as a ruthless employer of others to do his deadly work, no longer troubled by his conscience, with his ambition achieved. Then there is another supernatural encounter. Macbeth holds a banquet with the noble thanes to celebrate his kingship. Shakespeare shows the contrast in Macbeth before and after seeing Banquo's ghost, from being pleased and confident to frightened and determined to hold on to power at any cost. In all of this, he is supported, even saved, by the actions of Lady Macbeth.

1. Which is the last line in the scene where you think Macbeth is still confident and in control?
2. Choose three lines from the scene where you think Macbeth is gradually losing confidence and control.
3. What does Lady Macbeth say and do here to show a very quick grasp of the situation and the ability to take control of events?

② Characterisation and voice: dramatic language

An actor's voice is his or her most important asset. Tone of voice makes a huge difference to what an audience understands by hearing. An actor needs several 'voices' to convey different aspects of a character, and this means more than shouting in anger or whispering in fear. Here the actor playing Macbeth has to use at least five kinds of voice. What we see is Shakespeare's understanding of how speech reveals our thoughts and feelings.

4. What do you think is the difference between Macbeth's voice when welcoming guests and his voice when speaking to the murderer? Which words suggest his state of mind?
5. What is the difference between the voice he uses to speak to Banquo's ghost and the voice to speak to Lady Macbeth?
6. What kind of voice does he use to plan at the end of the scene?
7. How does Shakespeare's script help the actor playing Lady Macbeth to use different kinds of voice when talking to her husband and when talking to the guests?

③ Themes and ideas

Three themes in this scene are of supernatural influence, Macbeth's increasing violence, and the support of Lady Macbeth.

8. How does this scene show that Macbeth's fears about 'consequences' and 'the life to come' (Act 1 Scene 7 lines 1–7) were not just nervousness?
9. How does Shakespeare show Macbeth's increasing brutality and abuse of power in this scene? Pick out key words that show this.
10. Lady Macbeth supports and saves Macbeth here but Shakespeare gives signs at the end that he is beginning to act independently without her support and encouragement. What are they? Think about what he does, says, and how he says it.

EXAMINER'S NOTES, 3.4

4 Performance

The way that a scene is staged makes a huge difference to what the audience understands from seeing. The setting is the most obvious part of this – does it establish a realistic social setting? The presence of other actors, including non-speaking ones, is also important.

11 How do the initial stage directions and opening lines to 'Thanks to your majesty' create a realistic and formal setting on stage?

12 How does Shakespeare create a mood of relaxing dinner-party company before the arrival of Banquo's ghost? Pick out two phrases to support your answer.

13 What would you advise actors to do during Macbeth's speech to the ghost? Think about Macbeth's behaviour and the words he uses.

14 What would be the most effective way of showing the exit of the guests at the end of the scene? Think about what Lady Macbeth says and does.

15 How would you advise the staging of Banquo's Ghost? For example: use the same actor who played Banquo? a white shroud effect? a lighting spotlight? sound effects? bloody wounds? Give reasons for your opinions.

5 Contexts and responses

There are various ways in which different audiences may react to this scene, depending on whether they feel sorrow for the murdered Banquo or sympathy with Macbeth who has got what he wanted but finds things already going wrong.

16 A Jacobean audience would more easily accept that Macbeth was seeing a real ghost because of a greater belief in supernatural matters. Do you think it better for a modern audience to have no ghost on stage, to suggest that Macbeth is imagining it? Give reasons for your opinions.

17 Does Lady Macbeth's covering up for her husband make her seem more of a ruthless, scheming woman or a supportive partner with quick wits and more ability to manage than her husband? Explain your opinion.

6 Reflecting on the scene

18 In what ways does Shakespeare show different aspects of Macbeth and Lady Macbeth through the ways they speak in this scene? Track through what they say and how they say it.

19 What does this scene show about Shakespeare's understanding of the themes of ambition, guilt and the supernatural?

20 How could performance of this scene make some people feel sympathetic to Macbeth and others feel that he has lost all rights to sympathy?

ACT 3 SCENE 5

Thunder. Enter three Witches, meeting Hecate.

First Witch   Why, how now Hecate, you look angerly.

Hecate

Have I not reason, beldams, as you are?
Saucy and overbold, how did you dare
To trade and traffic with Macbeth,
In riddles and affairs of death?   5
And I, the mistress of your charms,
The close contriver of all harms,
Was never called to bear my part,
Or show the glory of our art?
And which is worse, all you have done   10
Hath been but for a wayward son,
Spiteful and wrathful who, as others do,
Loves for his own ends, not for you.
But make amends now. Get you gone,
And at the pit of Acheron   15
Meet me i' th' morning. Thither he
Will come to know his destiny.
Your vessels and your spells provide,
Your charms and everything beside.
I am for th' air. This night I'll spend   20
Unto a dismal and a fatal end.
Great business must be wrought ere noon.
Upon the corner of the moon
There hangs a vap'rous drop, profound,
I'll catch it ere it come to ground;   25
And that distilled by magic sleights,
Shall raise such artificial sprites,
As by the strength of their illusion,
Shall draw him on to his confusion.
He shall spurn fate, scorn death, and bear   30
His hopes 'bove wisdom, grace and fear.
And you all know, security
Is mortals' chiefest enemy.

Music and a song.

Hark, I am called. My little spirit, see,
Sits in a foggy cloud and stays for me.   *[Exit Hecate.]* 35

A song within, "Come away, come away" etc.

First Witch   Come, let's make haste; she'll soon be back again.

Exit the three Witches.

ACT 3 SCENE 6

Enter Lennox and another Lord.

Lennox

My former speeches have but hit your thoughts
Which can interpret farther. Only I say
Things have been strangely borne. The gracious Duncan

SHAKESPEARE'S WORLD

Shakespeare probably didn't write this scene. When Shakespeare's company, the King's Men, put an old play on again, they often added some new scenes, so more people would come to watch it again. After Shakespeare died another playwright, Thomas Middleton, revised *Macbeth* for the King's Men. Middleton probably added two songs and a dance to *Macbeth*. Hecate's song 'Come, away…' is also in Middleton's play *The Witch* (1616).

1 **Hecate:** goddess of the moon and witchcraft
2 **beldams:** witches
3 **trade and traffic:** have dealings with
6 **charms:** spells, magic
7 **close contriver:** secret arranger
11 **wayward son:** unreliable ally (Macbeth)
15 **pit of Acheron:** part of Hell
16 **Thither:** There
18 **vessels:** containers (their cauldron)
21 **Unto a dismal … end:** planning something evil and deadly
22 **wrought:** done
24 **vap'rous drop:** foggy drop said to be from the moon to be used in spells
25 **profound:** so full it is about to fall to Earth
26 **distilled by magic sleights:** strengthened by magic skills
27 **artificial sprites:** unreal spirits
28 **illusion:** ability to trick
29 **confusion:** ruin, overthrow
30 **spurn:** reject
30–1 **bear His hopes 'bove:** hopes that make him act against
32 **security:** feeling confident, safe
32 **mortals:** humans
35 **stays:** waits

1–2 **My former speeches … farther:** we are in agreement
3 **been strangely borne:** turned out oddly

74

Was pitied of Macbeth, marry, he was dead.
And the right valiant Banquo walked too late,   5
Whom, you may say (if't please you) Fleance killed,
For Fleance fled. Men must not walk too late.
Who cannot want the thought, how monstrous
It was for Malcolm and for Donalbain
To kill their gracious father? Damnèd fact,   10
How it did grieve Macbeth! Did he not straight
In pious rage, the two delinquents tear,
That were the slaves of drink and thralls of sleep?
Was not that nobly done? Ay, and wisely too.
For 'twould have angered any heart alive   15
To hear the men deny't. So that I say
He has borne all things well. And I do think
That had he Duncan's sons under his key,
(As, an't please heaven, he shall not) they should find
What 'twere to kill a father. So should Fleance.   20
But peace, for from broad words, and 'cause he failed
His presence at the tyrant's feast, I hear
Macduff lives in disgrace. Sir, can you tell
Where he bestows himself?

Lord   The son of Duncan,   25
From whom this tyrant holds the due of birth,
Lives in the English court, and is received
Of the most pious Edward with such grace,
That the malevolence of fortune nothing
Takes from his high respect. Thither Macduff   30
Is gone, to pray the holy king upon his aid
To wake Northumberland and warlike Siward.
That, by the help of these (with Him above
To ratify the work) we may again
Give to our tables meat, sleep to our nights,   35
Free from our feasts and banquets bloody knives,
Do faithful homage and receive free honours,
All which we pine for now. And this report
Hath so exasperate the king that he
Prepares for some attempt of war.   40

Lennox   Sent he to Macduff?

Lord   He did. And with an absolute "Sir, not I."
The cloudy messenger turns me his back,
And hums, as who should say, "You'll rue the time
That clogs me with this answer."   45

Lennox   And that well might
Advise him to a caution, t'hold what distance
His wisdom can provide. Some holy angel
Fly to the court of England and unfold
His message ere he come, that a swift blessing   50
May soon return to this our suffering country
Under a hand accursed.

Lord   I'll send my prayers with him.

Exit Lennox and the Lord.

---

8 **want the thought:** help thinking

10 **fact:** action (the murder)
11 **straight:** at once
12 **pious:** loyal, devoted
12 **two delinquents:** Duncan's servants
13 **thralls:** prisoners

17 **borne:** done
18 **under his key:** locked up
19 **an't:** if it
21 **from broad words:** because he spoke what he thought, unguardedly
21–2 **failed his presence … feast:** he didn't go to Macbeth's banquet
24 **bestows himself?:** is staying
26 **holds:** withholds, keeps away from
26 **due of birth:** the crown he should have inherited
28 **pious Edward:** King Edward the Confessor, known for his devotion to religion
28 **grace:** kindness, favour
29 **malevolence of fortune:** loss of his kingdom
29–30 **nothing Takes from … respect:** hasn't stopped him being treated with great respect
31 **upon his aid:** to help Malcolm
32 **wake:** call to war
33 **Him above:** God
34 **ratify:** approve
36 **Free from:** remove from
37 **Do faithful … free honours:** show loyalty to a king who will reward us for it
38 **pine:** long for
39 **exasperate:** angered
39 **the king:** Macbeth
43 **cloudy:** unhappy
43 **turns … back:** turns away
44–5 **hums, as … answer":** as if he wanted to say, "you'll regret that answer"
47 **Advise him to a caution:** warn Macduff to take care
47–8 **t'hold what distance … provide:** to keep as far from Macbeth as possible
52 **Under a hand accursed:** ruled by a hateful king (Macbeth)

Thunder. Enter the three Witches.

First Witch   Thrice the brinded cat hath mewed.

Second Witch   Thrice, and once the hedge-pig whined.

Third Witch   Harpier cries — 'Tis time, 'tis time.

First Witch   Round about the cauldron go:
In the poisoned entrails throw.
Toad, that under cold stone
Days and nights has thirty-one,
Sweltered venom sleeping got,
Boil thou first i' th' charmèd pot!

All   Double, double, toil and trouble;   10
Fire burn, and cauldron bubble.

Second Witch   Fillet of a fenny snake,
In the cauldron boil and bake.
Eye of newt, and toe of frog,
Wool of bat, and tongue of dog,   15
Adder's fork, and blind-worm's sting,
Lizard's leg, and howlet's wing.
For a charm of powerful trouble,
Like a hell-broth, boil and bubble.

All   Double, double, toil and trouble,   20
Fire burn, and cauldron bubble.

Third Witch   Scale of dragon, tooth of wolf,
Witch's mummy, maw and gulf

5

1 **Thrice:** Three times
1 **brinded:** striped
2 **hedge-pig:** hedgehog
3 **Harpier:** the third witch's 'familiar' – her link to the world of magic, disguised as an animal
5 **entrails:** guts
8 **Sweltered venom:** poison, sweated by the toad
9 **sleeping got:** taken while it slept
12 **Fillet:** a thick slice of
12 **fenny:** from the Fens, which are marshy and muddy
15 **Wool:** hair
16 **fork:** tongue
16 **blind-worm:** slow-worm
17 **howlet:** young owl
23 **mummy:** a powder made from Egyptian mummies
23 **maw and gulf:** throat and stomach

The Witches, spring 2010.

The First Witch is in the centre. What are the other two Witches doing? Quote from the text to support your answer.

l–r Rachel Winters, Karen Bryson, Shane Zaza

Of the ravined salt-sea shark,
Root of hemlock, digged i' th' dark, 25
Liver of blaspheming Jew,
Gall of goat, and slips of yew
Slivered in the moon's eclipse,
Nose of Turk, and Tartar's lips,
Finger of birth-strangled babe 30
Ditch-delivered by a drab,
Make the gruel thick and slab.
Add thereto a tiger's chaudron,
For th' ingredients of our cauldron.

All   Double, double, toil and trouble, 35
Fire burn, and cauldron bubble.

Second Witch   Cool it with a baboon's blood,
Then the charm is firm and good.

Enter Hecate, and three other Witches.

Hecate   O well done! I commend your pains,
And every one shall share i' th' gains. 40
And now about the cauldron sing,
Like elves and fairies in a ring,
Enchanting all that you put in.

*Music, they sing a song, putting in more ingredients as they
dance round the cauldron.*

Second Witch   By the pricking of my thumbs,
Something wicked this way comes. 45

Exit Hecate and the other three witches.

Open, locks, whoever knocks!

Enter Macbeth.

Macbeth   How now, you secret, black and midnight hags?
What is't you do?

All   A deed without a name.

Macbeth   I conjure you, by that which you profess,
Howe'er you come to know it, answer me. 50
Though you untie the winds and let them fight
Against the churches, though the yeasty waves
Confound and swallow navigation up,
Though bladed corn be lodged, and trees blown down,
Though castles topple on their warders' heads 55
Though palaces and pyramids do slope
Their heads to their foundations, though the treasure
Of nature's germens tumble all together,
Even till destruction sicken. Answer me
To what I ask you. 60

First Witch   Speak.

Second Witch   Demand.

Third Witch   We'll answer.

24 **ravined:** full to bursting
25 **hemlock:** a poisonous plant
26 **blaspheming:** denying Christian beliefs
27 **Gall:** bitter liquid from the liver
27 **slips:** small twigs
28 **Slivered:** cut
29–30 **Turk ... Tartar ... birth-strangled babe:** none of these were baptised Christian, so the Witches could use them
31 **Ditch-delivered:** born in a ditch
31 **drab:** prostitute
32 **slab:** sticky
33 **chaudron:** guts

39 **commend your pains:** praise you for the trouble you have taken

49 **conjure:** demand

51 **Though:** Even if
51–2 **untie ... churches:** send storms to knock down churches
52 **yeasty:** frothy
53 **Confound:** smash up
53 **navigation:** ships at sea
54 **bladed corn be lodged:** ripening corn is blown flat (and so ruined)
55 **warders:** people in charge
56 **slope:** bend
57–8 **the treasure ... all together:** the elements that bring life itself are thrown into chaos
59 **sicken:** feels sick with overeating

SHAKESPEARE'S WORLD

Stage traps

In this scene, Shakespeare uses the trapdoor. This was a door in the floor of the stage, which led to an area underneath the stage. Actors or props (such as the witches' cauldron) could come up through the trapdoor. In Shakespeare's time, the trapdoor was often used for the appearance of ghosts and devils, so it had a strong association with Hell or the Underworld. By using the trapdoor here, Shakespeare was hinting that the Witches were supernatural beings.

Macbeth and one of the apparitions, spring 2010.

This effect was made with a large sheet of black silk, which, with an actor inside it, came out of the stage trap. What might the two Witches in the background be doing to solve a practical problem?

James Garnon

FROM THE REHEARSAL ROOM...

STATUS

- As a whole group, each person will be given a card from 1–10. When you get your card, you cannot look at it, but hold it above your head so that the rest of the room can clearly see your number.
- The number on the cards will indicate the status of the person – 1 being the lowest and 10 the highest.
- Your aim is to walk around the room and try to work out your own status. Greet people according to their status, and they will greet you according to yours. Make sure that the greetings are simple such as 'hello' and that you use eye contact and body language in your greeting.
- Try to greet everyone.
- When told, the whole group should line up according to what status number you think you

are. Note that more than one person may have the same status.

1. What clues made you choose the status you thought you were?

2. Status is something that is not only played, but also is given to us.

   a) How did you give people high or low status?

   b) How does this happen in everyday life?

   c) Who, in *Macbeth*, has high status but is made low status by other characters?

3. Read through Act 4 Scene 1, from the entrance of Macbeth (line 46, page 77) to the entrance of Lennox (line 138, page 82).

   a) Who has the highest and lowest status in this scene? Quote from the text to support your answer.

   b) What in the language suggests this? Does the status change at any point? Why?

First Witch	Say, if th' hadst rather hear it from our mouths,	
	Or from our masters?	65
Macbeth	Call 'em. Let me see 'em.	
First Witch	Pour in sow's blood that hath eaten	
	Her nine farrow, grease that's sweaten	
	From the murderer's gibbet, throw	
	Into the flame.	70
All	Come high or low:	
	Thyself and office deftly show!	*Thunder.*

An Apparition appears, it is a head wearing armour.

Macbeth	Tell me, thou unknown power.	
First Witch	He knows thy thought.	
	Hear his speech, but say thou naught.	
1st Apparition	Macbeth, Macbeth, Macbeth! Beware Macduff!	75
	Beware the Thane of Fife! Dismiss me. Enough.	

1st Apparition descends.

Macbeth	Whate'er thou art, for thy good caution, thanks.	
	Thou hast harped my fear aright. But one word more.	
First Witch	He will not be commanded. Here's another,	
	More potent than the first.	*Thunder.* 80

2nd Apparition appears, it is a bloody child.

2nd Apparition	Macbeth, Macbeth, Macbeth!	
Macbeth	Had I three ears, I'd hear thee.	
2nd Apparition	Be bloody, bold, and resolute. Laugh to scorn	
	The power of man, for none of woman born	
	Shall harm Macbeth.	85

2nd Apparition descends.

Macbeth	Then live Macduff: what need I fear of thee?	
	But yet I'll make assurance double sure,	
	And take a bond of fate. Thou shalt not live,	
	That I may tell pale-hearted fear it lies,	
	And sleep in spite of thunder.	*Thunder.*

3rd Apparition appears, it is a child, crowned, with a tree in its hand.

Macbeth	What is this	90
	That rises like the issue of a king,	
	And wears upon his baby-brow the round	
	And top of sovereignty?	
All Witches	Listen, but speak not to't.	
3rd Apparition	Be lion-mettled, proud, and take no care	
	Who chafes, who frets, or where conspirers are.	95
	Macbeth shall never vanquish'd be, until	
	Great Birnam wood to high Dunsinane hill	
	Shall come against him.	

Glossary

68 **farrow:** piglets
69 **sweaten:** sweated
69 **gibbet:** post that murders were hung from

72 **Thyself and office:** you and your role
72 **deftly:** skilfully

78 **harped:** guessed

80 **potent:** powerful

83 **resolute:** determined
84 **none:** no one

87 **make assurance double sure:** kill him anyway, to be on the safe side
88 **take a bond of fate:** make sure fate keeps its promise
89 **That I may:** so that I will be able to

91 **issue:** child
92–3 **round And top of sovereignty:** crown

94 **lion-mettled:** brave as a lion
95 **chafes:** argues, resists
95 **frets:** is unhappy with your reign
96 **vanquish'd:** defeated

Macbeth and the apparitions of the kings, spring 2010.

How has the director chosen to stage this differently to the way the text suggests? Suggest reasons why he might have done this.

James Garnon

Actor's view

Rachel Winters
Third Witch, spring 2010

In this scene, [and] I think right from the start of the play, they never actually have control over Macbeth, it's all about the power of suggestion. They suggest things, and OK so they tell him, this is going to happen to you, and he chooses to believe these things. They see this before this particular scene, and they see that he is going along with what they are saying, that he's tempted by it all. And when they meet him in this particular scene they know — well, he's already killed the king, he's killed Banquo, so they know they've got him. It's a funny one. [He comes in thinking he's in charge, but] he's the one who is asking all the questions and they choose to answer him, which shows, I think, that they are in control. At the end of the scene they are saying, 'seek to know no more'. Actually, we are not going to tell you any more. That's it. They are in control.

Actor's view

Janet Fullerlove
First Witch, summer 2010

When Macbeth comes in at the beginning of this scene, when we've been casting a spell and plotting, it is all very much part of our plan. We want Macbeth back. That's what the spell is all about. We start to cast, for us, the ultimate spell. This is the one where we want to get him, hook, line and sinker. We're calling him back almost. So when he comes in we're almost playing it as though we're surprised:, "Oh, it's you!" There is a point where he walks forward and says, "I want you to answer my questions". We're almost playing it with our back to him, as though we're going to not go there, and then we eventually say "Speak. Demand. We'll answer". That's when we think "Okay, now we've got him, we've really sucked him in here, he's coming all the way, we're going to take him right to the depths of this, he's going to be horrified by what we show him."

3rd Apparition descends.

Macbeth   That will never be.
Who can impress the forest, bid the tree
Unfix his earth-bound root? Sweet bodements, good!
Rebellious dead, rise never till the wood
Of Birnam rise, and our high-placed Macbeth
Shall live the lease of nature, pay his breath
To time and mortal custom. Yet my heart
Throbs to know one thing. Tell me, if your art
Can tell so much: shall Banquo's issue ever
Reign in this kingdom?

All Witches   Seek to know no more.

Macbeth   I will be satisfied. Deny me this,
And an eternal curse fall on you. Let me know —

The cauldron descends. Music (oboes) offstage.

Why sinks that cauldron? And what noise is this?   110

First Witch   Show.

Second Witch   Show.

Third Witch   Show.

All Witches   Show his eyes, and grieve his heart;
Come like shadows, so depart.

*A procession of eight kings, the last holding a mirror,
followed by the Ghost of Banquo. They move past Macbeth
during his next speech.*

Macbeth   Thou are too like the spirit of Banquo. Down!
Thy crown does sear mine eyeballs. And thy hair,
Thou other gold-bound brow, is like the first.
A third, is like the former. — Filthy hags!
Why do you show me this? — A fourth? Start, eyes!   120
What, will the line stretch out to th' crack of doom?
Another yet!? A seventh? I'll see no more.
And yet the eighth appears, who bears a glass
Which shows me many more. And some I see
That twofold balls and treble sceptres carry.   125
Horrible sight! Now I see 'tis true,
For the blood-boltered Banquo smiles upon me,
And points at them for his.

[The procession has left the stage.]

                What? Is this so?

First Witch   Ay sir, all this is so. But why
Stands Macbeth thus amazedly?   130
Come sisters, cheer we up his sprites,
And show the best of our delights.
I'll charm the air to give a sound,
While you perform your antic round.
That this great king may kindly say,   135
Our duties did his welcome pay.

---

99 **impress:** force to join an army

100 **bodements:** predictions
101 **Rebellious dead:** Banquo

103–4 **the lease of nature ... mortal custom:** his given life-span, dying naturally

105 **art:** skills

115 **so:** in the same way

117 **sear:** burn
118 **gold-bound brow:** crowned head
119 **former:** one before
120 **Start:** burst from your sockets
121 **th' crack of doom:** the Day of Judgement (when God sends the dead to Heaven or Hell)

125 **twofold balls ... sceptres carry:** carrying the symbols of a ruler, but twice, to show he rules two countries, as King James ruled England and Scotland at the time
127 **blood-boltered:** smothered in blood
128 **for his:** as his descendants

130 **amazedly:** stunned
131 **sprites:** spirits

134 **antic round:** unnatural dance
136 **Our ... pay:** we treated him respectfully and did as he asked

81

Music. The Witches dance, then vanish.

Macbeth   Where are they? Gone? Let this pernicious hour
Stand aye accursèd in the calendar. —
Come in, without there!   *Enter Lennox.*

Lennox   What's your grace's will?

Macbeth   Saw you the weird sisters?

Lennox   No, my lord.   140

Macbeth   Came they not by you?

Lennox   No indeed, my lord.

Macbeth   Infected be the air whereon they ride,
And damned all those that trust them! — I did hear
The galloping of horse. who was't came by?

Lennox   'Tis two or three, my lord, that bring you word.   145
Macduff is fled to England.

Macbeth   Fled to England?

Lennox   Ay, my good lord.

Macbeth   Time, thou anticipat'st my dread exploits.
The flighty purpose never is o'ertook   150
Unless the deed go with it. From this moment,
The very firstlings of my heart shall be
The firstlings of my hand. And even now
To crown my thoughts with acts, be it thought and done
The castle of Macduff I will surprise,   155
Seize upon Fife; give to th' edge o' th' sword
His wife, his babes, and all unfortunate souls
That trace him in his line. No boasting like a fool,
This deed I'll do, before this purpose cool.
But no more sights. — Where are these gentlemen?   160
Come bring me where they are.

Exit Macbeth and Lennox.

137 **pernicious:** dangerous
138 **aye:** forever

139 **Come in, without there!:**
calling Lennox who is waiting
outside
149 **anticipat'st:** have guessed
149 **dread exploits:** fearsome deeds
150–1 **The flighty ... with it:**
Planning a deed isn't enough –
you have to do it quickly
152–3 **The very firstlings ... hand:**
From now on I must act as soon
as I think of a deed
154 **crown:** follow through
155 **surprise:** attack without warning
156 **Fife:** the area Macduff rules
156 **give to ... sword:** kill
158 **trace him in his line:** are his
descendants
159 **before this purpose cool:** at
once
160 **sights:** visions

Director's Note, 4.1

- ✔ Macbeth visits the Witches.
- ✔ They show him visions which reassure him, but include 'beware Macduff'.
- ✔ He asks about Banquo, and is dismayed by a vision of many descendents of Banquo as kings.
- ✔ Shaken by this, and by the news that Macduff has fled, he decides to have Macduff's family killed.
- ✔ What effect do the visions have on Macbeth?

EXAMINER'S NOTES, 4.1

1 Character and plot development

The first time Macbeth met the Witches, they chose to meet him. This time he is more firmly in their power as he seeks them out to tell him his future. At first, he is anxious to know what they can tell him. By the end, he is confident and believes he can make himself even safer by extending his rule by terror.

1 Macbeth says he will go to the Witches, yet they know he is coming before they see him. What makes the audience realise this?

2 Originally there were three Witches. The audience now becomes aware of a greater force. How many Witches are there? How are the Witches presented here?

3 Although Macbeth told his wife he would go to see the Witches, he did not bring her with him. Why do you think Macbeth has not brought his wife with him to see the Witches?

2 Characterisation and voice: dramatic language

The Witches' speech is detailed and suggestive of their links with death. Their shared speech is a rhythmic chorus that makes them seem united in a familiar ritual. Macbeth's language reflects his changing feeling. His voice alternates between commanding, questioning and exclamations of dismay.

4 When Macbeth arrives he thinks he can interrogate or command the supernatural creatures. What words, phrases and tone suggest this?

5 How is Macbeth's amazement, disappointment and uncertainty conveyed by the way he speaks in lines 108–128? Pick out words and punctuation to support your observations.

6 Which words and tone suggest that Macbeth is confident again and feels in charge of his life in this last speechs, lines 149–161?

7 How does Shakespeare show a contrast between the Witches who seem a group reciting a ritual and Macbeth?

These questions help you to explore many aspects of *Macbeth*. At GCSE, your teacher will tell you which aspects are relevant to how your Shakespeare response will be assessed.

EXAMINER'S TIP

A good response

A good response may refer to effects on the character on stage and then to effects on people in the audience.

For example, the effect of this scene on Macbeth is that he is more confident at the end because he thinks he has received some good news.

The effect on the audience is that we think that he is mistaken in his new confidence, and has been cheated.

Surrounded by the audience: an evening performance of *Macbeth*, summer 2010.

EXAMINER'S TIP

Writing about drama

Sometimes the success of a performance comes from what the audience sees, not just what it hears. Writing about visual business such as cauldrons descending into trap doors, or dances, or illusions, shows you are aware of Shakespeare's use of varied techniques to keep the audience interested.

USING THE VIDEO

Exploring interpretation and performance

If you have looked at the video extracts in the online version try these questions.

- The Witches emerge from the dining table used in the last scene and carry it off. Do you think this is a neat way of removing the props or can it be seen as a way of making the Witches seem capable of interfering and transforming everything around them?

- Macbeth enters through the audience and speaks many of his lines directly to them. Might this might make them more sympathetic to him or less?

EXAMINER'S TIP

Reflecting on the scene

Writing about the Witches' voices, or Macbeth as a victim, or dramatic techniques, can be helped by referring to the way your understanding has developed by seeing a performance on stage or screen, or performing an aspect of the scene yourself or as part of a group.

3 **Themes and ideas**

The theme of power is developed to show that the supernatural power that seemed to favour Macbeth is not there for his service. He cannot command the apparitions, who appear to offer good news but encourage false security. They seem hostile to Macbeth who seems a victim of their evil power.

8 What makes the audience realise that Macbeth cannot control these supernatural forces?

9 How do we realise that the Witches do not feel any loyalty to or sympathy with Macbeth?

10 What, in Macbeth's first speech, shows that the Witches do harm, not just to sailors and farmers and kings, but to religion, too?

4 **Performance**

Staging this scene demands sound effects, apparitions that appear and disappear, music, dance – a feast of spectacle with foul ingredients. It's a scene to keep the audience gripped with horror, disgust and fear.

11 How do stage directions in the scene help to create atmosphere?

12 The ingredients for the cauldron signal malice and danger: how many references to poisonous substances are there?

13 How would you suggest presenting the three apparitions on stage or on screen?

14 How could the actor playing Macbeth bring out the difference in his feelings between his speech in lines 116–129 and lines 149–161?

15 What can you find in the script and the stage directions to prompt theatrically exciting audio and visual effects?

5 **Contexts and responses**

Shakespeare's audience would have been less influenced by a scientific view of the world, and more likely to have a strong religious faith.

16 A Jacobean audience might view Macbeth as a victim of supernatural forces more readily than today's audience. Do you think Macbeth is a victim, or are they reinforcing what was in him anyway?

17 Among the disgusting and dangerous ingredients of the cauldron, Shakespeare includes the liver of a Jew and the nose of a Turk and the lips of a Tartar (i.e. non-Christians). How may a Jacobean audience have responded to these items differently from a modern audience?

6 **Reflecting on the scene**

18 How do the voices of the Witches bring out their savage, deadly and deceiving nature?

19 How does Shakespeare's writing of this scene make the audience aware that Macbeth, although strong, is a victim of evil forces beyond his control?

20 How does Shakespeare exploit dramatic techniques to create a powerful theatrical experience in this scene?

Enter Lady Macduff, her son, and Ross.

Lady Macduff   What had he done, to make him fly the land?

Ross   You must have patience, madam.

Lady Macduff   He had none.
His flight was madness. When our actions do not,
Our fears do make us traitors.

Ross   You know not
Whether it was his wisdom, or his fear.   5

Lady Macduff   Wisdom? To leave his wife, to leave his babes,
His mansion and his titles, in a place
From whence himself does fly? He loves us not.
He wants the natural touch, for the poor wren,
The most diminutive of birds, will fight,   10
Her young ones in her nest, against the owl.
All is the fear, and nothing is the love;
As little is the wisdom, where the flight
So runs against all reason.

Ross   My dearest coz,   15
I pray you, school yourself. But for your husband,
He is noble, wise, judicious, and best knows
The fits o' th' season. I dare not speak much further,
But cruel are the times, when we are traitors
And do not know ourselves. When we hold rumour   20
From what we fear, yet know not what we fear,
But float upon a wild and violent sea
Each way and move. — I take my leave of you:
Shall not be long but I'll be here again.
Things at the worst will cease or else climb upward   25
To what they were before.   *[To the son.]*

My pretty cousin,
Blessing upon you!

Lady Macduff   Fathered he is, and yet he's fatherless.

Ross   I am so much a fool, should I stay longer
It would be my disgrace and your discomfort.   30
I take my leave at once.   *Exit Ross.*

Lady Macduff   Sirrah, your father's dead,
And what will you do now? How will you live?

Son   As birds do, mother.

Lady Macduff   What, with worms and flies?

Son   With what I get, I mean, and so do they.

Lady Macduff   Poor bird, thou'dst never fear the net, nor lime,   35
The pit-fall, nor the gin.

Son   Why should I, mother?
Poor birds they are not set for.
My father is not dead, for all your saying.

3–4 **When our actions … traitors:**
even the innocent can seem guilty
if fear makes them run away

8 **From whence:** from which
9 **wants the natural touch:** lacks
human feelings
10 **most diminutive:** smallest
12 **All is the fear … love:** his fear
has overcome his love for his
family
14 **runs against all reason:** makes
no sense
15 **coz:** cousin (used for close
relative or friend)
16 **school:** control
18 **fits o' th' season:** violent
changes of these times
20 **And do not know ourselves:**
without realising it
20-1 **hold rumour From what we
fear:** are driven by fear to believe
rumours
23 **Each way and move:** tossed in
all directions
25 **climb upward:** improve

30 **It would be … discomfort:**
I would embarrass us both by
weeping
31 **Sirrah:** Boy

35–6 **lime … pit-fall … gin:** traps

38 **Poor birds … set for:** they are
only set for important people

85

Lady Macduff, children and a servant.

1 At what point during the text on the opposite page was this picture taken? Quote form the text to support your answer.
2 Look back at the stage directions on page 85. What has the director added to this scene?
3 What effect on the audience do you think she intended this change to have?

l–r (foreground) Mia Adams, Simone Kirby, Charlie George

Lady Macduff	Yes, he is dead. How wilt thou do for father?	40
Son	Nay, how will you do for a husband?	
Lady Macduff	Why, I can buy me twenty at any market.	
Son	Then you'll buy 'em to sell again.	
Lady Macduff	Thou speak'st with all thy wit, And yet, i' faith, with wit enough for thee.	45
Son	Was my father a traitor, mother?	
Lady Macduff	Ay, that he was.	
Son	What is a traitor?	
Lady Macduff	Why, one that swears and lies.	
Son	And be all traitors that do so?	50
Lady Macduff	Everyone that does so is a traitor, and must be hanged.	
Son	And must they all be hang'd that swear and lie?	
Lady Macduff	Every one.	
Son	Who must hang them?	
Lady Macduff	Why, the honest men.	55
Son	Then the liars and swearers are fools. For there are liars and swearers enough to beat the honest men and hang up them.	
Lady Macduff	Now God help thee, poor monkey. But how wilt thou do for a father?	60
Son	If he were dead, you'd weep for him. If you would not, it were a good sign that I should quickly have a new father.	
Lady Macduff	Poor prattler, how thou talk'st!	

Enter Messenger.

Messenger	Bless you, fair dame. I am not to you known, Though in your state of honor I am perfect. I doubt some danger does approach you nearly. If you will take a homely man's advice, Be not found here. Hence with your little ones. To fright you thus, methinks I am too savage: To do worse to you were fell cruelty, Which is too nigh your person. Heaven preserve you, I dare abide no longer. *Exit Messenger.*	65 70
Lady Macduff	Whither should I fly? I have done no harm. But I remember now I am in this earthly world: where to do harm Is often laudable, to do good sometime Accounted dangerous folly. Why then, alas, Do I put up that womanly defence, To say I have done no harm? *Enter Murderers.*	75
	What are these faces?	80

44 **wit:** intelligence

49 **swears and lies:** makes a promise under oath and breaks it (but her son thinks she means ordinary swearing and lying)
50 **be all traitors ... so?:** are all who do that traitors?

64 **prattler:** chatterbox

66 **in your state ... perfect:** I know your status and reputation
67 **doubt:** suspect
67 **nearly:** close by
68 **homely:** simple, ordinary
69 **Hence:** away from here
70-1 **To fright you ... fell cruelty:** I'm sorry to scare you with this warning, but it would be even crueller not to warn you
72 **nigh:** near
73 **abide:** stay

77 **laudable:** worthy of praise
78 **Accounted:** considered to be
78 **folly:** stupidity

Director's Note, 4.2

✔ Ross visits Lady Macduff. She cannot understand why Macduff has left his family in Scotland.

✔ We see a happy family, but they are interrupted, first by a warning, then by the Murderers.

✔ What effect does this scene have on the audience?

FROM THE REHEARSAL ROOM...

WHAT YOU THINK AND WHAT YOU SAY

- In pairs read through the *Working Cut* for the dialogue between Lady Macduff and her son.

- Now read through the *Working Cut* again. This time before you say each line, say aloud (in your own words) what you think your character is thinking. Remember, the trick is not to translate the line they say, but to think about what they mean.

1 How different did you think the character's thoughts were, from what they said?

2 Did this change the way you said your line?

3 In this dialogue, do Lady Macduff and her son say what they are thinking?

Working Cut – text for experiment

L.'duff	Sirrah, your father's dead, And what will you do now? How will you live?
Son	As birds do, mother.
L.'duff	What, with worms and flies?
Son	With what I get, I mean, and so do they. My father is not dead, for all your saying.
L.'duff	Yes, he is dead. How wilt thou do for father?
Son	Nay, how will you do for a husband?
L.'duff	Why, I can buy me twenty at any market.
Son	Then you'll buy 'em to sell again.
L.'duff	Thou speak'st with all thy wit,
Son	Was my father a traitor, mother?
L.'duff	Ay, that he was.
Son	What is a traitor?
L.'duff	Why, one that swears and lies.
Son	And be all traitors that do so?
L.'duff	Everyone that does so is a traitor, and must be hanged.
Son	And must they all be hang'd that swear and lie?
L.'duff	Every one.
Son	Who must hang them?
L.'duff	Why, the honest men.
Son	Then the liars and swearers are fools.
L.'duff	Now God help thee, poor monkey.
Son	If he were dead, you'd weep for him.
L.'duff	Poor prattler, how thou talk'st!

Murderer	Where is your husband?	
Lady Macduff	I hope in no place so unsanctified Where such as thou may'st find him.	82 **unsanctified:** unholy
Murderer	He's a traitor.	
Son	Thou liest, thou shag-eared villain!	84 **shag-eared:** with cut ears (some crimes were punished by ear cutting)
Murderer	What, you egg? *[Stabbing him.]* Young fry of treachery!	85 **Young fry of treachery!:** Son of a traitor!
Son	He has kill'd me, mother: 85 Run away, I pray you! *[He dies.]*	

Exit Lady Macduff, crying 'Murder', pursued by the Murderers, one of whom takes the son's body.

ACT 4 SCENE 3

Enter Malcolm and Macduff.

Malcolm	Let us seek out some desolate shade, and there Weep our sad bosoms empty.	1 **desolate shade:** lonely place
Macduff	Let us rather Hold fast the mortal sword, and like good men, Bestride our downfall'n birthdom. Each new morn 5 New widows howl, new orphans cry, new sorrows Strike heaven on the face, that it resounds As if it felt with Scotland, and yelled out Like syllable of dolour.	4 **fast:** tightly 4 **mortal:** deadly 5 **Bestride our downfall'n birthdom:** defend the fallen country of our birth 7 **that:** so that 9 **Like syllable of dolour:** the same miserable cries
Malcolm	What I believe, I'll wail; 10 What know, believe; and what I can redress, As I shall find the time to friend, I will. What you have spoke, it may be so perchance. This tyrant, whose sole name blisters our tongues, Was once thought honest. You have loved him well, 15 He hath not touched you yet. I am young, but something You may discern of him through me, and wisdom To offer up a weak, poor innocent lamb To appease an angry god.	10 **wail:** weep over 11 **redress:** put right 12 **As I shall ... will:** At the most favourable time 13 **perchance:** perhaps 14 **sole name:** name alone 16–7 **something You may ... through me:** you might see the difference between us 18–9 **To offer up ... god:** to hand me over to him to keep him happy
Macduff	I am not treacherous.	
Malcolm	But Macbeth is. 20 A good and virtuous nature may recoil In an imperial charge. But I shall crave your pardon. That which you are, my thoughts cannot transpose. Angels are bright still, though the brightest fell. Though all things foul would wear the brows of grace, 25 Yet grace must still look so.	21–2 **recoil In an imperial charge:** give way to a king's demands 23 **transpose:** change into something else 24 **the brightest fell:** the brightest angel, Lucifer, rebelled and became the Devil 25–6 **Though all things foul ... look so:** Evil people try to seem good, but don't forget that those who are good also seem good
Macduff	I have lost my hopes.	
Malcolm	Perchance even there where I did find my doubts.	

A

Macduff, summer 2010

Both photos were taken during part of this scene covered by the text on pages 91 and 93.

1 At what point might Macduff look at Macolm as he does in photo A? Quote to support your answer.

2 Which character is threatening the other in photo B? Quote to support your answer.

Macolm and Macduff, spring 2010

A: Keith Dunphy
B: Philip Cumbus, Nicholas Khan

B

	Why in that rawness left you wife and child,	
	(Those precious motives, those strong knots of love),	30
	Without leave-taking? I pray you,	
	Let not my jealousies be your dishonours,	
	But mine own safeties. You may be rightly just,	
	Whatever I shall think.	

Macduff   Bleed, bleed, poor country!   35
Great tyranny, lay thou thy basis sure,
For goodness dare not check thee. Wear thou thy wrongs,
The title is affeerrd. Fare thee well, lord,
I would not be the villain that thou think'st
For the whole space that's in the tyrant's grasp   40
And the rich East to boot.

Malcolm   Be not offended.
I speak not as in absolute fear of you.
I think our country sinks beneath the yoke,
It weeps, it bleeds, and each new day a gash   45
Is added to her wounds. I think withal
There would be hands uplifted in my right,
And here from gracious England have I offer
Of goodly thousands. But, for all this,
When I shall tread upon the tyrant's head,   50
Or wear it on my sword, yet my poor country
Shall have more vices than it had before;
More suffer, and more sundry ways than ever,
By him that shall succeed.

Macduff   What should he be?

Malcolm   It is myself I mean, in whom I know   55
All the particulars of vice so grafted,
That when they shall be opened, black Macbeth
Will seem as pure as snow, and the poor state
Esteem him as a lamb, being compared
With my confineless harms.   60

Macduff   Not in the legions
Of horrid hell can come a devil more damned
In evils to top Macbeth.

Malcolm   I grant him bloody,
Luxurious, avaricious, false, deceitful,   65
Sudden, malicious, smacking of every sin
That has a name. But there's no bottom, none,
In my voluptuousness. Your wives, your daughters,
Your matrons, and your maids, could not fill up
The cistern of my lust, and my desire   70
All continent impediments would o'erbear,
That did oppose my will. Better Macbeth
Than such an one to reign.

Macduff   Boundless intemperance
In nature is a tyranny. It hath been   75
Th' untimely emptying of the happy throne,

29 **in that rawness:** unprotected
30 **motives:** reasons for doing things
31 **leave-taking:** permission to go from the king
32 **jealousies be your dishonours:** suspicions seem to suggest you are dishonourable
33 **But mine own safeties:** I'm concerned for my own safety
33 **rightly just:** completely honest
36-7 **lay thou ... check thee:** you can get a strong grip on the country, when good people don't dare to stop you
37-8 **Wear thou ... title is affeerrd:** You don't need to hide your evil deeds, your claim to the throne is confirmed
40 **the whole space:** all the land (Scotland)
41 **to boot:** too
44 **sinks beneath the yoke:** is dragged down by Macbeth's tyranny
46 **withal:** also
47 **hands uplifted ... right:** people willing to fight to make me king of Scotland
48 **gracious England:** the English king
51 **wear it on my sword:** cut it off and show it on the end of my sword
53 **more sundry ways:** in different ways
54 **What should he be?:** who do you mean?
56-7 **All the particulars ... be opened:** have so many vices that when you know them
59 **Esteem:** value
60 **confineless harms:** limitless evils
61 **legions:** armies
63 **top:** go further than
65 **Luxurious:** lustful
65 **avaricious:** greedy for wealth
66 **Sudden:** unpredictable
66 **smacking of:** touched by
68 **voluptuousness:** desire for pleasure
69 **matrons:** older (usually married) women
70 **fill up ... lust:** satisfy me
71 **All continent ... o'erbear:** would force anyone
74 **Boundless intemperance:** wild lack of self-control
76 **Th' ... throne:** the cause of many a king losing his throne

TRUST

- **A**, you are the leader of one group of friends. You have secret plans. You are visited by **B**, a member of a rival group.
- **A** thinks **B** would like to join **A**'s group, but you are not sure if you can trust him/her.
- **A**, welcome **B** into your house, and improvise a conversation with **B**. The whole aim of this conversation is to find out if you can trust **B**.
- **B**, you want to prove you are trustworthy. How would you do this?

1 Make a list of the tactics **A** used.

2 Make a list of the tactics **B** used.

- **A**, you will play Malcolm.
- **B**, you will play Macduff.
- Read the *Working Cut*. You will find that your improvisation mirrors what happens in this scene.

3 What tactics from your list can you see Malcolm and Macduff using in this scene?

- Read the *Working Cut* again, emphasising these tactics.

4 How does Shakespeare show us Malcolm might be a good king? Support your answer with quotes from the text.

Working Cut – text for experiment

Malc	Let us seek out some desolate shade, and there Weep our sad bosoms empty. This tyrant, whose sole name blisters our tongues, Was once thought honest. You have loved him well.
Macd	I am not treacherous.
Malc	But Macbeth is. That which you are, my thoughts cannot transpose. Angels are bright still, though the brightest fell. Why in that rawness left you wife and child, Without leave-taking?
Macd	Bleed, bleed, poor country! The title is affeerd. Fare thee well, lord, I would not be the villain that thou think'st.
Malc	Be not offended. When I shall tread upon the tyrant's head, Or wear it on my sword, yet my poor country Shall have more vices than it had before; More suffer, and more sundry ways than ever, By him that shall succeed.

Macd	What should he be?
Malc	It is myself I mean, in whom I know All the particulars of vice so grafted, That when they shall be opened, black Macbeth Will seem as pure as snow, and the poor state Esteem him as a lamb, being compared With my confineless harms.
Macd	Not in the legions Of horrid hell can come a devil more damned In evils to top Macbeth.
Malc	I grant him bloody, Luxurious, avaricious, false, deceitful, Sudden, malicious, smacking of every sin That has a name. But there's no bottom, none, In my voluptuousness. Your wives, your daughters, Your matrons, and your maids, could not fill up The cistern of my lust. Better Macbeth Than such an one to reign.
Macd	O Scotland, Scotland!
Malc	If such a one be fit to govern, speak. I am as I have spoken.
Macd	Fit to govern? No, not to live. O nation miserable! These evils thou repeat'st upon thyself Have banished me from Scotland. O my breast, Thy hope ends here!
Malc	Macduff, this noble passion, Child of integrity, hath from my soul Wiped the black scruples, reconciled my thoughts To thy good truth and honour. I am yet Unknown to woman, never was forsworn, Scarcely have coveted what was mine own, My first false speaking was this upon myself. What I am truly is my poor country's to command.

Actor's view

Philip Cumbus
Malcolm, spring 2010

Malcolm has a wonderful self-awareness that I think the other characters do not have. I think by the virtue of the fact that he has imagined himself to be the worst king of all kings, the fact that he is aware enough to think that that is possible within himself, means that I think he'll be all right. I think he's got enough integrity and enough foresight to see where the bad path would lead so that that path can be avoided, as opposed to people like Macbeth. So I think Malcolm has enough foresight to be able to avoid some of the traps that were laid before him. So I think he might be all right.

And fall of many kings. But fear not yet
To take upon you what is yours. You may
Convey your pleasures in a spacious plenty,
And yet seem cold. The time you may so hoodwink.   80
We have willing dames enough. There cannot be
That vulture in you, to devour so many
As will to greatness dedicate themselves,
Finding it so inclined.

Malcolm   With this, there grows
In my most ill-composed affection, such   85
A staunchless avarice, that were I king,
I should cut off the nobles for their lands.
Desire his jewels, and this other's house,
And my more-having would be as a sauce
To make me hunger more, that I should forge   90
Quarrels unjust against the good and loyal,
Destroying them for wealth.

Macduff   This avarice
Sticks deeper; grows with more pernicious root
Than summer-seeming lust, and it hath been
The sword of our slain kings. Yet do not fear;   95
Scotland hath foisons to fill up your will
Of your mere own. All these are portable,
With other graces weighed.

Malcolm   But I have none. The king-becoming graces,
As justice, verity, temp'rance, stableness,   100
Bounty, perseverance, mercy, lowliness,
Devotion, patience, courage, fortitude,
I have no relish of them, but abound
In the division of each several crime,
Acting it many ways. Nay, had I power, I should   105
Pour the sweet milk of concord into hell,
Uproar the universal peace, confound
All unity on earth.

Macduff   O Scotland, Scotland!

Malcolm   If such a one be fit to govern, speak.   110
I am as I have spoken.

Macduff   Fit to govern?
No, not to live. O nation miserable!
With an untitled tyrant bloody-sceptered,
When shalt thou see thy wholesome days again?   115
Since that the truest issue of thy throne
By his own interdiction stands accursed
And does blaspheme his breed? Thy royal father
Was a most sainted king. The queen that bore thee,
Oft'ner upon her knees than on her feet,   120
Died every day she lived. Fare thee well.
These evils thou repeat'st upon thyself
Have banished me from Scotland. O my breast,
Thy hope ends here!

79–80 **Convey your pleasures … hoodwink:** take your pleasure secretly, tricking people into thinking you are pure

83–4 **As will to … inclined:** as would happily sleep with a king if he wanted it

85 **ill-composed affection:** evil nature

86 **staunchless avarice:** unstoppable greed

87 **cut off:** kill

89–90 **my more-having … more:** the more I took, the more I would want

90 **that:** so that

90 **forge:** make, invent

93–4 **more … summer-seeming lust:** more deeply-rooted, harder to stop than youthful

95 **sword of our slain kings:** caused the death on many kings

96 **foisons:** enough wealth

97 **Of your mere own:** just from your royal possessions

97 **these:** these vices

97 **portable:** bearable

98 **With other graces weighed:** set against your good points

99 **king-becoming graces:** virtues a king should have

100 **As:** such as

100 **verity:** truthfulness

100 **temp'rance:** self-restraint

101 **Bounty:** generosity

101 **lowliness:** humility, lack of pride

102 **Devotion:** love of God

102 **fortitude:** endurance

103 **relish:** taste for, enjoyment of

103–5 **abound In the division … many ways:** enjoy committing sin in many different ways

106 **concord:** peace, harmony

107 **Uproar:** throw into confusion

107 **confound:** disrupt

114 **untitled:** with no right to rule

115 **wholesome:** healthy

116 **truest issue of thy throne:** person with most right to be king

117 **interdiction:** accusation

118 **does blaspheme his breed:** dishonours his family

121 **Died every day she lived:** daily prayed for forgiveness to be sure of going to heaven when she died

122–3 **These evils … Scotland:** your confession has destroyed any hope I had of returning to Scotland

Malcolm, Macduff (hidden by Malcolm) and Ross, summer 2010.

Crowns, hanging from chains, rotated round the stage during this scene. Why might the director have chosen to do this?

James McArdle and Julius D'Silva

Malcolm Macduff, this noble passion, 125
Child of integrity, hath from my soul
Wiped the black scruples, reconciled my thoughts
To thy good truth and honour. Devilish Macbeth,
By many of these trains, hath sought to win me
Into his power, and modest wisdom plucks me 130
From over-credulous haste. But God above
Deal between thee and me. For even now
I put myself to thy direction, and
Unspeak mine own detraction. Here abjure
The taints and blames I laid upon myself, 135
For strangers to my nature. I am yet
Unknown to woman, never was forsworn,
Scarcely have coveted what was mine own,
At no time broke my faith, would not betray
The devil to his fellow, and delight 140
No less in truth than life. My first false speaking
Was this upon myself. What I am truly
Is thine and my poor country's to command.
Whither, indeed, before thy here-approach,
Old Siward with ten thousand warlike men 145
Already at a point, was setting forth.
Now we'll together; and the chance of goodness
Be like our warranted quarrel. Why are you silent?

Macduff Such welcome and unwelcome things at once

Enter a Doctor.

'Tis hard to reconcile. Well, more anon. — 150
Comes the king forth, I pray you?

Doctor Ay, sir. There are a crew of wretched souls
That stay his cure. Their malady convinces
The great assay of art. But at his touch,
Such sanctity hath heaven given his hand, 155
They presently amend.

Malcolm I thank you, doctor.   *Exit Doctor.*

Macduff What's the disease he means?

Malcolm 'Tis called the evil.
A most miraculous work in this good king, 160
Which often, since my here-remain in England,
I have seen him do. How he solicits heaven
Himself best knows, but strangely-visited people
All swoll'n and ulcerous, pitiful to the eye,
The mere despair of surgery, he cures, 165
Hanging a golden stamp about their necks,
Put on with holy prayers. And 'tis spoken,
To the succeeding royalty he leaves
The healing benediction. With this strange virtue,
He hath a heavenly gift of prophecy, 170
And sundry blessings hang about his throne,
That speak him full of grace.

---

126 **Child of integrity:** born of your honest nature
127 **black scruples:** sinister doubts
127-8 **reconciled my thoughts … truth and honour:** convinced me you are honest
129 **by many of these trains:** sending people to say what Macduff has said to Malcolm to trick him into going back to Scotland
130-1 **modest wisdom … haste:** I have to be careful who I believe
133 **to thy direction:** in your hands
134 **Unspeak mine own detraction:** take back my accusations against myself
134 **abjure:** deny
135 **taints and blames … myself:** sins I accused myself of
136 **For strangers to my nature:** as totally unlike me
137 **Unknown to woman:** a virgin
137 **was forsworn:** broke an oath
138 **Scarcely have coveted … own:** have hardly even desired my own possessions
139 **my faith:** a solemn promise
141 **false speaking:** lie
144 **Whither:** Where (to Scotland)
144 **here-approach:** arrival here
146 **at a point:** ready for battle
147-8 **chance of goodness … quarrel:** may we be as successful as our reason for fighting is right
150 **Such welcome … reconcile:** I have heard two such different stories – one welcome, the other not – that it is hard to know what to think
153 **stay his cure:** wait for him to cure them
153-6 **Their malady … amend:** They have a disease that they believe God has given him the power to cure by touch
159 **the evil:** scrofula
161 **here-remain:** stay here
162 **solicits:** gets help from
163 **strangely-visited:** those with the disease
166 **stamp:** coin
167 **Put on with holy prayers:** which he has prayed over
168-9 **To the succeeding … benediction:** his descendants will inherit this power

Macduff, Ross (in black at the back of the stage), and Malcolm, spring 2010.

This photograph was taken between line 190 and line 230.

1 Are the characters where you would expect them to be on the stage? Explain your answer.

2 It was the Director's choice to isolate Macduff on stage. How might it affect the way the audience reacts to Macduff? Give reasons for your answer.

⊢ Nicholas Khan, Pieter Lawman, Philip Cumbus

Enter Ross.

Macduff	See, who comes here?
Malcolm	My countryman, but yet I know him not.
Macduff	My ever-gentle cousin, welcome hither.
Malcolm	I know him now. Good God betimes remove
	The means that makes us strangers.
Ross	Sir, amen
Macduff	Stands Scotland where it did?
Ross	Alas poor country,
	Almost afraid to know itself. It cannot
	Be called our mother, but our grave, where nothing
	But who knows nothing, is once seen to smile.
	Where sighs and groans and shrieks that rent the air
	Are made, not marked. Where violent sorrow seems
	A modern ecstasy. The dead man's knell
	Is there scarce asked for who, and good men's lives
	Expire before the flowers in their caps,
	Dying or ere they sicken.
Macduff	O relation
	Too nice, and yet too true!
Malcolm	What's the newest grief?
Ross	That of an hour's age doth hiss the speaker,
	Each minute teems a new one.
Macduff	How does my wife?
Ross	Why well.
Macduff	And all my children?
Ross	Well too.
Macduff	The tyrant has not battered at their peace?
Ross	No, they were well at peace, when I did leave 'em.
Macduff	Be not a niggard of your speech. How goes't?
Ross	When I came hither to transport the tidings,
	Which I have heavily borne, there ran a rumour
	Of many worthy fellows that were out,
	Which was to my belief witnessed the rather,
	For that I saw the tyrant's power a-foot.
	Now is the time of help. Your eye in Scotland
	Would create soldiers, make our women fight,
	To doff their dire distresses.
Malcolm	Be't their comfort
	We are coming thither. Gracious England hath
	Lent us good Siward and ten thousand men,
	An older and a better soldier none
	That Christendom gives out.
Ross	Would I could answer

175

180

185

190

195

200

205

210

173 but … not: but I don't recognise him

176 The means … strangers: the separation that makes strangers of us

177 Stands … did?: Is the situation in Scotland unchanged?

180–1 nothing … to smile: where only those who don't know what is going on can be cheerful
182 rent: tear, split
183 Are … marked: are not even commented on
184 modern ecstasy: everyday emotion
184–5 The … who: people hardly bother to ask who the funeral bell is ringing for
186 Expire: die, end
187 or ere they sicken: before
188 O relation … true: The details of this account are awful, but, sadly, all too accurate
189 nice: accurate
191 That of an hour's … speaker: what happened an hour ago is old news
192 teems a new one: is filled with new examples

199 Be not a niggard … speech: tell the whole story
200 tidings: news
201 heavily borne: have found hard to bear
202 out: prepared for battle
203–4 to my belief … a-foot: I was ready to believe because Macbeth's army was on the march
205 eye: arrival, being seen
207 doff their dire distresses: get rid of their miseries (Macbeth's rule)

210–1 An older … out: There's no better soldier in the whole Christian world
212 Would: I wish

A

Macduff (on the left in photo A) and Ross, summer 2010.

These photos were taken while the text on pages 97 and 99 was being performed. Which photo was taken first? Quote from the text to support your answer.

Julius D'Silva and Keith Dunphy

B

	This comfort with the like. But I have words That would be howled out in the desert air, Where hearing should not latch them.
Macduff	What concern they? The general cause? Or is it a fee-grief Due to some single breast?
Ross	No mind that's honest But in it shares some woe, though the main part Pertains to you alone.
Macduff	If it be mine, Keep it not from me, quickly let me have it.
Ross	Let not your ears despise my tongue for ever, Which shall possess them with the heaviest sound That ever yet they heard.
Macduff	H'm: I guess at it.
Ross	Your castle is surprised. Your wife and babes Savagely slaughtered. To relate the manner Were, on the quarry of these murdered deer To add the death of you.
Malcolm	Merciful heaven! What, man, ne'er pull your hat upon your brows. Give sorrow words. The grief that does not speak Whispers the o'er-fraught heart and bids it break.
Macduff	My children too?
Ross	Wife, children, servants, all that could be found.
Macduff	And I must be from thence? My wife killed too?
Ross	I have said.
Malcolm	Be comforted. Let's make us med'cines of our great revenge, To cure this deadly grief.
Macduff	He has no children. — All my pretty ones? Did you say all? — O hell-kite! — All? What, all my pretty chickens and their dam At one fell swoop?
Malcolm	Dispute it like a man.
Macduff	I shall do so. But I must also feel it as a man. I cannot but remember such things were That were most precious to me. Did heaven look on, And would not take their part? Sinful Macduff, They were all struck for thee! Naught that I am, Not for their own demerits, but for mine, Fell slaughter on their souls. Heaven rest them now.
Malcolm	Be this the whetstone of your sword. Let grief Convert to anger. Blunt not the heart, enrage it

Line numbers: 215, 220, 225, 230, 235, 240, 245, 255

Glossary:

213 **the like:** equally cheering news
215 **latch:** catch
217 **The general cause:** the fate of Scotland
217-8 **fee-grief … breast:** bad news for just one person
219-20 **No mind that's … some woe:** any honest person shares the trouble
221 **Pertains:** belongs
224 **possess:** tell
227 **is surprised:** has been attacked without warning
228-30 **To relate … you:** If I were to tell you how, it would kill you too
232 **ne'er pull … brows:** don't hide your face
234 **Whispers the o'er-fraught:** whispers to the over-loaded
244 **dam:** mother
245 **fell:** deadly
245 **Dispute:** Deal with
250 **take their part:** act to save them
251 **Naught that:** worthless as
252 **demerits:** faults, failings
254 **whetstone:** a tool used to sharpen blades
255 **Blunt not the heart:** don't shut down your feelings

A

B

Director's Note, 4.3

✔ Macduff joins Malcolm in England. At first Malcolm thinks this might be a plot to betray him to Macbeth.

✔ Malcolm decides to trust Macduff, and tells him he has an English army ready to invade Scotland.

✔ Ross arrives with news from Scotland. He tells Macduff his family has been murdered.

✔ What impression of Macbeth as a king do we get in this scene?

Lady Macbeth watched by her gentlewoman and the Doctor, summer 2010.

1 What words would you use to describe photo A?

2 What words would you use to describe photo B?

3 What have the directors and actors done to give these different impressions?

Above, *l–r* Laura Rogers, Janet Fullerlove, Ian Pirie; below, Eve Best

Lady Macbeth, 2001.

SHAKESPEARE'S WORLD
◇◇◇◇◇◇◇◇◇◇◇◇◇

The Waiting Gentlewoman

In Shakespeare's day, the Queen's waiting gentlewomen were members of the court. They came from noble families, often with strong royal connections. Although she was a servant, a gentlewoman did not clean or cook for the family. She was a companion. She might read to, or play music for her mistress. At times, a waiting woman might even advise her mistress on the latest dress, dances and music fashionable at the time. Waiting women often knew family secrets, since they lived in close quarters with the family, as does Lady Macbeth's gentlewoman in this scene.

Macduff	O, I could play the woman with mine eyes And braggart with my tongue. — But gentle heavens, Cut short all intermission. Front to front Bring thou this fiend of Scotland and myself. Within my sword's length set him, if he 'scape, 260 Heaven forgive him too.
Malcolm	This tune goes manly. Come, go we to the king, our power is ready, Our lack is nothing but our leave. Macbeth Is ripe for shaking, and the powers above 265 Put on their instruments. Receive what cheer you may, The night is long, that never finds the day.

Exit all.

256 **play the woman ... eyes:** weep
257 **braggart with my tongue:** boast of the revenge I'll take
258 **Cut short all intermission:** don't leave time for that
258 **Front to front:** face to face
262 **tune goes:** way of speaking is
263 **power:** army
264 **Our lack is ... leave:** All we have left to do is say farewell to King Edward
265 **ripe for shaking:** at a point where he can be pushed from the throne
266 **Put on their instruments:** are getting ready too

ACT 5 SCENE 1

Enter a Doctor of Physic and a Waiting-Gentlewoman.

Doctor	I have two nights watched with you, but can perceive no truth in your report. When was it she last walked?
Gentlewoman	Since his majesty went into the field, I have seen her rise from her bed, throw her nightgown upon her, unlock her closet, take forth paper, fold it, write upon't, 5 read it, afterwards seal it, and again return to bed; yet all this while in a most fast sleep.
Doctor	A great perturbation in nature, to receive at once the benefit of sleep, and do the effects of watching. In this slumbery agitation, besides her walking and other 10 actual performances, what (at any time) have you heard her say?
Gentlewoman	That, sir, which I will not report after her.
Doctor	You may to me, and 'tis most meet you should.
Gentlewoman	Neither to you, nor any one, having no witness to 15 confirm my speech.

Enter Lady Macbeth, in her nightgown, with a candle.

	Lo you, here she comes. This is her very guise, and upon my life, fast asleep. Observe her, stand close.
Doctor	How came she by that light?
Gentlewoman	Why it stood by her. She has light by her continually, 20 'tis her command.
Doctor	You see her eyes are open.
Gentlewoman	Ay but their sense are shut.
Doctor	What is it she does now? Look how she rubs her hands. 25
Gentlewoman	It is an accustomed action with her, to seem thus washing her hands. I have known her continue in this a quarter of an hour.

3 **went into the field:** led his army off to fight the rebels
5 **closet:** private storage box
8 **perturbation in nature:** disturbance of her normal state of mind
8 **at once:** at the same time
9 **do the effects of watching:** act as if awake
10 **slumbery agitation:** sleepwalking
11 **actual performances:** things you have actually seen her do
13 **report after her:** repeat
14 **meet:** suitable, right

17 **her very guise:** the way she behaved before
18 **stand close:** don't let her see you

23 **their sense are shut:** they don't see

26 **accustomed:** usual (when she sleepwalks)

LADY MACBETH

- In groups of three, read through Act 5 Scene 1.
- In this scene, Lady Macbeth refers to some past events. In your group decide what events she is referring to, and find the scenes in the play where these events take place.

1 What does Lady Macbeth remember? You should both quote what she says from the text, and explain why that refers to the previous action in the play.

2 The audience sees a different side to Lady Macbeth in this scene. The audience has not seen Lady Macbeth since the end of the banquet. Since then, what has happened to her state of mind? Quote from the text to support your answer.

Actor's view

Laura Rogers
Lady Macbeth, summer 2010

[This scene] is a challenge in itself, purely because, from an actor's point of view, you have been off stage for such a long time – the last thing they see of you is the banquet scene.

Before the sleep-walking scene you've had huge sleep deprivation, so you feel that you're going slightly insane as well and because when you do sleep you just have these images in your head. So, it's a brilliant scene for an actress to play because it does allow you to play it in any way you like because people react to madness differently. It felt very freeing. Obviously, you know, I don't suffer from sleep-walking myself and I'm not aware of anyone that does. So, you just have to put yourself in that position. It's written so well for you. The challenge, I suppose, is, like any challenge at the Globe, that you can see the audience. And so you have to just imagine that there's nobody there, and how you would behave if you thought there was nobody witnessing it. But, I think, for me that was one of my favourite scenes. Once you get yourself into that place, then there's nothing you can't do with that scene. And the director and I talked about it. I suppose it could be played incredibly manic, but she [Lucy Bailey, the director] said that she wanted the audience to really sympathise with the character at this point, and just see the scared little girl come out. That she's done this terrible thing but [she] does regret; she can never go back and take that moment back. And what's it's doing to her mind. [Lucy] wanted to see somebody that almost died from the inside. And so, hopefully, the audience did.

Lady Macbeth, spring 2010.

1 Pick a line from the text opposite that Lady Macbeth might have been saying as the photo was taken. Quote from the text to support your answer.

2 Compare this photo, from the spring 2010 production, with the two photos on page 100 (summer 2010 at the top of the page, and 2001 at the bottom).

a) In what ways did each production suggest Lady Macbeth was sleepwalking?

b) In what way did each production suggest Lady Macbeth was a woman in a crisis?

c) If you were directing *Macbeth*, or playing Lady Macbeth, how would you stage this scene?

Claire Cox

Lady Macbeth	Yet here's a spot.
Doctor	Hark, she speaks. I will set down what comes from her, to satisfy my remembrance the more strongly.
Lady Macbeth	Out damned spot! Out I say! One: Two: why then 'tis time to do't. Hell is murky. Fie, my lord, fie, a soldier, and afeard? What need we fear? Who knows it, when none can call our power to account? Yet who would have thought the old man to have had so much blood in him?
Doctor	Do you mark that?
Lady Macbeth	The Thane of Fife, had a wife: where is she now? What, will these hands ne'er be clean? No more o' that my lord, no more o' that. You mar all with this starting.
Doctor	Go to, go to. You have known what you should not.
Gentlewoman	She has spoke what she should not, I am sure of that. Heaven knows what she has known.
Lady Macbeth	Here's the smell of the blood still. All the perfumes of Arabia will not sweeten this little hand. Oh, oh, oh!
Doctor	What a sigh is there! The heart is sorely charged.
Gentlewoman	I would not have such a heart in my bosom for the dignity of the whole body.
Doctor	Well, well, well.
Gentlewoman	Pray God it be, sir.
Doctor	This disease is beyond my practice. Yet I have known those which have walked in their sleep, who have died holily in their beds.
Lady Macbeth	Wash your hands, put on your nightgown, look not so pale. I tell you yet again Banquo's buried; he cannot come out on's grave.
Doctor	Even so?
Lady Macbeth	To bed, to bed. There's knocking at the gate. Come, come, come, come, give me your hand. What's done, cannot be undone. To bed, to bed, to bed.

Exit Lady Macbeth.

Doctor	Will she go now to bed?
Gentlewoman	Directly.
Doctor	Foul whisperings are abroad. Unnatural deeds Do breed unnatural troubles. Infected minds To their deaf pillows will discharge their secrets. More needs she the divine than the physician. God, God, forgive us all. Look after her,

30

35

40

45

50

55

60

65

70

30 **set:** write
31 **to satisfy my ... strongly:** so I will remember it more accurately
32 **One: Two:** counting the striking of a bell

35 **none can call ... account:** we'll be so powerful no one can accuse us

38 **mark:** hear

39 **Thane of Fife:** Macduff

41 **You mar all ... starting:** Your nervous behaviour will ruin everything

49 **sorely charged:** weighed down with grief

51 **dignity of the whole body:** position of queen

54 **beyond my practice:** too difficult for my skills to cure
55–6 **who have died ... beds:** and it has not killed them

59 **on's:** of his

60 **Even so?:** So that's it?

65 **Directly:** straight away

66 **Foul whisperings are abroad:** There are terrible rumours being spread

69 **divine:** priest (to confess her sins to)

Lennox, Menteith and a soldier, summer 2010.

The director has decided this is towards the end of a campaign, and there has been fighting already.

1 How can you tell this, from what you can see in the photograph?

2 Is there any justification in the text for the director's decision? Quote to support your answer.

_l_ Nick Court, _r_ Michael Clamp

FROM THE REHEARSAL ROOM...

REPORTS ABOUT MACBETH

- In groups of four, read through Act 5 Scene 2.
- List all the words and phrases that the Scottish lords use to describe Macbeth.
- As a group, decide how Macbeth is being observed by his enemies, and create a _freeze frame_ to represent this.

1 What words and images are used to describe Macbeth?

2 Do the lords consider Macbeth to be a strong or weak opponent? Give reasons for your answer.

Director's Note, 5.2

- ✔ An army of Scottish rebels is close to meeting up with Malcolm, Macduff, and the English forces.
- ✔ They report that Macbeth has few supporters, and he has fortified himself in Dunsinane Castle.
- ✔ What is significant about Macbeth's choice?

Remove from her the means of all annoyance,
And still keep eyes upon her. So, good-night,
My mind she has mated, and amazed my sight.
I think, but dare not speak.

Gentlewoman Good-night, good doctor.   *They exit.* 75

*Enter soldiers: a drummer, and others with flags. Then
enter Menteith, Caithness, Angus, Lennox, and more
Soldiers.*

Menteith The English power is near, led on by Malcolm,
His uncle Siward, and the good Macduff.
Revenges burn in them, for their dear causes
Would to the bleeding and the grim alarm
Excite the mortified man.   5

Angus Near Birnam Wood
Shall we well meet them, that way are they coming.

Caithness Who knows if Donalbain be with his brother?

Lennox For certain, sir, he is not. I have a file
Of all the gentry; there is Siward's son   10
And many unrough youths, that even now
Protest their first of manhood.

Menteith What does the tyrant?

Caithness Great Dunsinane he strongly fortifies.
Some say he's mad. Others, that lesser hate him,   15
Do call it valiant fury, but for certain
He cannot buckle his distempered cause
Within the belt of rule.

Angus   Now does he feel
His secret murders sticking on his hands,
Now minutely revolts upbraid his faith-breach.   20
Those he commands move only in command,
Nothing in love. Now does he feel his title
Hang loose about him, like a giant's robe
Upon a dwarfish thief.

Menteith   Who then shall blame
His pestered senses to recoil and start,   25
When all that is within him does condemn
Itself for being there?

Caithness   Well, march we on,
To give obedience where 'tis truly owed.
Meet we the med'cine of the sickly weal,
And with him pour we in our country's purge,   30
Each drop of us.

Lennox   Or so much as it needs,
To dew the sovereign flower, and drown the weeds.
Make we our march towards Birnam. *Exit all, marching.*

---

71 **the means of all annoyance:** anything she could harm herself with
73 **mated:** bewildered

Director's Note, 5.1

✔ Lady Macbeth is watched as she sleepwalks by her Gentlewoman and a Doctor.
✔ She seems to wash her hands, and talks about the murders she has been involved in.
✔ The Gentlewoman and Doctor are scared by what they have heard.
✔ What has happened to Lady Macbeth?

3 **their dear causes:** the wrongs they are revenging
4–5 **to the bleeding ... man:** rouse even a dead man to fight for them
7 **well:** have the advantage if we
9 **file:** list
10 **gentry:** people of good birth (in the army)
11–2 **unrough youths ... manhood:** young men in battle for the first time
15 **lesser hate him:** don't hate him as much
16 **valiant fury:** warlike rage
17–8 **buckle his distempered ... rule:** use the fact he's king to justify his present actions
20 **minutely revolts ... faith-breach:** now there are new rebellions every minute because of his disloyalty (to Duncan and Scotland)
21–2 **move only in command ... love:** obey orders, but don't fight fiercely out of love for him
25 **pestered:** frantic
25 **to recoil and start:** for making him jumpy
26–7 **all that is within ... there?:** he hates himself for what he has become?
29 **the med'cine ... sickly weal:** the medicine that will cure Scotland (Malcolm)
30 **purge:** medicine that cleans the stomach and bowels
32 **dew the sovereign ... weeds:** support the proper ruler (Malcolm) and get rid of these who shouldn't be there (Macbeth and his supporters)

Macbeth in Act 5 Scene 3, summer 2010.

1 Read the scene. Is the other actor in the picture more likely to be the Servant, or Seyton? Quote from the text to support your answer.

2 Sticking with your answer to Question 1, pick a line from the text to use as a caption for this photograph, and explain why you have chosen it.

l Elliot Cowan, *r* Gareth Bennett-Ryan

ACT 5 SCENE 3

Enter Macbeth, Doctor, and Attendants.

Macbeth	Bring me no more reports, let them fly all.
	Till Birnam Wood remove to Dunsinane,
	I cannot taint with fear. What's the boy Malcolm?
	Was he not born of woman? The spirits that know
	All mortal consequences have pronounced me thus: 5
	"Fear not, Macbeth, no man that's born of woman
	Shall e'er have power upon thee." Then fly, false thanes,
	And mingle with the English epicures.
	The mind I sway by, and the heart I bear,
	Shall never sag with doubt, nor shake with fear. 10

Enter a Servant.

	The devil damn thee black, thou cream-faced loon!
	Where got'st thou that goose look?
Servant	There is ten thousand—
Macbeth	Geese, villain?
Servant	Soldiers sir. 15
Macbeth	Go prick thy face and over-red thy fear,
	Thou lily-livered boy. What soldiers, patch?
	Death of thy soul, those linen cheeks of thine
	Are counsellors to fear. What soldiers whey-face?
Servant	The English force, so please you. 20
Macbeth	Take thy face hence. *[Exit Servant.]*
	Seyton! — I am sick at heart,
	When I behold — Seyton, I say! — This push
	Will cheer me ever or dis-seat me now.
	I have lived long enough. My way of life
	Is fallen into the sear, the yellow leaf, 25
	And that which should accompany old age,
	As honour, love, obedience, troops of friends,
	I must not look to have. But in their stead,
	Curses, not loud but deep, mouth-honour, breath,
	Which the poor heart would fain deny, and dare not. — 30
	Seyton! *Enter Seyton.*
Seyton	What's your gracious pleasure?
Macbeth	What news more?
Seyton	All is confirmed, my lord, which was reported.
Macbeth	I'll fight till from my bones my flesh be hacked. 35
	Give me my armour.
Seyton	'Tis not needed yet.
Macbeth	I'll put it on.
	Send out more horses, skirr the country round,
	Hang those that talk of fear. Give me mine armour. —
	How does your patient, doctor? 40

1 **let them fly all:** I don't care if all my nobles desert me
3 **taint:** be stained, corrupted by
5 **All mortal consequences:** everything that will happen on earth
7 **false:** disloyal
8 **epicures:** lovers of luxury, people who live soft lives
9 **The mind I ... bear:** My mind and heart
11 **cream-faced loon:** white faced (with fear) useless, lazy, fool
12 **goose look:** frightened expression

16 **over-red thy fear:** spread the blood on your cheeks to hide your fear
17 **lily-livered:** cowardly
17 **patch:** fool
18 **linen:** white
19 **are counsellors to fear:** will make everyone else afraid
19 **whey-face:** milk-white

22 **push:** attack
23 **dis-seat me:** push me from my throne

25 **Is fallen ... leaf:** has reached its end, like a dry, yellow leaf
27 **As:** such as
28 **look to have:** expect, hope for
28 **stead:** place
29 **mouth-honour:** insincere flattery
29–30 **breath, Which ... not:** just air, words the speaker wishes he dared not to say

38 **skirr:** scour, search

A

A spectacular opening of Act 5 Scene 4, summer 2010.

From either side of the stage two groups of armed men sprinted towards each other, their weapons drawn, shouting fiercely.

In photo A you can see the English Army, led by Young Siward, Macduff, Ross, Malcolm and Old Siward.

In photo B you can see the back of the first of the Scottish Lords, and their army.

1 What is happening in photo C? Give reasons for your answer.

2 How does the director's choice in this case change the effect of the opening of the scene on the audience?

B

C

Doctor	Not so sick, my lord, As she is troubled with thick-coming fancies That keep her from her rest.
Macbeth	Cure her of that. Canst thou not minister to a mind diseased, Pluck from the memory a rooted sorrow; 45 Raze out the written troubles of the brain, And with some sweet oblivious antidote Cleanse the stuffed bosom of that perilous stuff Which weighs upon the heart?
Doctor	Therein the patient must minister to himself. 50
Macbeth	Throw physic to the dogs, I'll none of it. — Come, put mine armour on. Give me my staff. Seyton, send out. — Doctor, the Thanes fly from me. — Come sir, despatch. — If thou couldst, doctor, cast The water of my land, find her disease, 55 And purge it to a sound and pristine health, I would applaud thee to the very echo, That should applaud again. — Pull't off I say. — What rhubarb, senna, or what purgative drug, Would scour these English hence? Hear'st thou of them? 60
Doctor	Ay, my good lord. Your royal preparation Makes us hear something.
Macbeth	Bring it after me. I will not be afraid of death and bane, Till Birnam forest come to Dunsinane.
Doctor	*[Aside]* Were I from Dunsinane away and clear, 65 Profit again should hardly draw me here.

Exit all.

ACT 5 SCENE 4

Enter soldiers: a drummer, and others with flags. Then enter Malcolm, old Siward and his Son, Macduff, Menteith, Caithness, Angus, Lennox, Ross, and Soldiers marching.

Malcolm	Cousins, I hope the days are near at hand That chambers will be safe.
Menteith	We doubt it nothing.
Siward	What wood is this before us?
Meneith	The wood of Birnam. 5
Malcolm	Let every soldier hew him down a bough, And bear't before him, thereby shall we shadow The numbers of our host, and make discovery Err in report of us.
A Soldier	It shall be done.
Siward	We learn no other but the confident tyrant 10

41–2 Not so sick ... fancies: She's not really physically ill, but her mind cannot rest

44 minister to: treat, give medicine for

46 Raze out: erase

47 oblivious antidote: medicine to bring forgetfulness

48–9 the stuffed bosom ... heart?: her heart of the dangerous thoughts that fill it?

50 Therein: That is something

51 physic: medicine

52 staff: spear

54 despatch: hurry up

54–6 cast The ... pristine health: use your skill to diagnose Scotland's problems and cure them

58 Pull't off I say: (referring to his armour)

59–60 What rhubarb ... English hence?: What medicine would you prescribe to get rid of the English?

62 it: his armour

65 Were I: if only I was

66 Profit again ... me here: I wouldn't come back, no matter what you paid me

Director's Note, 5.3

We see Macbeth facing many problems:

✔ reports that the English Army is near at hand

✔ news from the Doctor of Lady Macbeth's illness.

How does Macbeth react to these problems?

2 chambers will be safe: we'll be able to sleep safe in our beds

3 We doubt it nothing: We don't doubt it

6 hew: cut

6 bough: branch

7 shadow: hide

8 host: army

8–9 discovery Err ... us: spies give wrong estimates of our numbers

10 We learn ... but: as far as we can tell

109

Malcolm, Macduff and Siward, summer 2010.

Which of them is speaking and what line might it be? Explain your answer.

l–r James McArdle, Keith Dunphy, Ken Shorter

Director's Note, 5.4

✔ The English army and the Scottish rebels have joined together.

✔ Malcolm orders the troops to cut down and carry branches from trees to hide the number of men he has.

✔ Malcolm's soldiers take trees from Birnam Wood, and they advance on Macbeth in his castle at Dunsinane.

✔ How does Macbeth react to this evidence of the Witches' prophesies coming true?

Actor's view

James Garnon
Macbeth, spring 2010

People say, about Lady Macbeth, "Oh she commits suicide". There is no evidence in the script that I can see that she does commit suicide. The only person who says that she commits suicide is Malcolm at the end, where he says "'Tis thought" she has killed herself. "'Tis thought" – I mean, it's not very categoric!

You know, Macbeth's reaction to her death is peculiar; he doesn't ask how she dies, he just sort of accepts it and gives this very peculiar speech. And I'd be more inclined to think something else has happened than that she's necessarily killed herself. Why do people believe Malcolm? I'm not sure.

FROM THE REHEARSAL ROOM...

LANGUAGE

- In groups of five read though the *Working Cut* text of this scene.

- One person reads Macbeth, and another person reads all the other parts.

- The other three people have listening tasks.

- **Person One** should listen out for repetition.

- **Person Two** should listen out for any mentions of time (day, night, hour etc).

- **Person Three** listens out for any imagery.

- When the Listeners hear what they are listening for (repetition, time or imagery), they repeat the words as soon as the Reader has said them.

1 What words are being repeated?

2 What time words are used? Why?

3 What images does Macbeth use?

4 What does repetition, the use of time words, and imagery tell us about Macbeth's state of mind in this scene?

Working Cut – text for experiment

Mac	Hang out our banners on the outward walls,
	Till famine and the ague eat them up.
[A cry of women within.]	
	What is that noise?
Sey	The queen, my lord, is dead.
Mac	She should have died hereafter;
	Tomorrow, and tomorrow, and tomorrow,
	Creeps in this petty pace from day to day,
	And all our yesterdays have lighted fools
	The way to dusty death. Out, out, brief candle.
[Enter a Messenger.]	
	Thou com'st to use thy tongue: thy story quickly.
Mess	As I did stand my watch upon the hill,
	I looked toward Birnam, and anon methought
	The wood began to move.
Mac	If thou speak'st false,
	Upon the next tree shalt thou hang alive,
	Till famine cling thee. I begin
	To doubt the' equivocation of the fiend
	That lies like truth. "Fear not, till Birnam wood
	Do come to Dunsinane", and now a wood
	Comes toward Dunsinane. – Arm, arm, and out!

	Keeps still in Dunsinane, and will endure Our setting down before't.
Malcolm	'Tis his main hope. For where there is advantage to be given, Both more and less have given him the revolt; And none serve with him but constrainèd things 15 Whose hearts are absent too.
Macduff	Let our just censures Attend the true event, and put we on Industrious soldiership.
Siward	The time approaches, 20 That will with due decision make us know What we shall say we have and what we owe. Thoughts speculative their unsure hopes relate, But certain issue, strokes must arbitrate. Towards which, advance the war. 25

Exit all, marching.

ACT 5 SCENE 5

Enter Macbeth, Seyton and soldiers: a drummer, and others with flags.

Macbeth	Hang out our banners on the outward walls, The cry is still, "They come:" Our castle's strength Will laugh a siege to scorn. Here let them lie Till famine and the ague eat them up. Were they not forced with those that should be ours, 5 We might have met them dareful, beard to beard, And beat them backward home.

A cry of women within.

What is that noise?

Seyton	It is the cry of women, my good lord. *[Exit.]*
Macbeth	I have almost forgot the taste of fears. The time has been, my senses would have cooled 10 To hear a night-shriek, and my fell of hair Would at a dismal treatise rouse and stir As life were in't. I have supped full with horrors, Direness, familiar to my slaughterous thoughts, Cannot once start me. *[Enter Seyton.]* Wherefore was that cry? 15
Seyton	The queen, my lord, is dead.
Macbeth	She should have died hereafter; There would have been a time for such a word. Tomorrow, and tomorrow, and tomorrow, Creeps in this petty pace from day to day, 20 To the last syllable of recorded time. And all our yesterdays have lighted fools The way to dusty death. Out, out, brief candle.

11-2 Keeps still ... before't: will be besieged rather than leave Dunsinane

13-4 where there is ... revolt: many common people and nobles have deserted him when they had the chance

15 constrainèd things: those forced to stay and fight

17-8 Let our just ... event: we can only know the truth of this when the battle's over

18-9 put we on ... soldiership: so we still need to fight hard and well

21 due decision: once its effects are assessed

22 What we shall say ... owe: how much of Scotland we truly possess

23-4 Thoughts speculative ... arbitrate: no point guessing and hoping, only fighting will give us the answer

4 famine and the ague: starvation and fever

5 forced with those ... ours: reinforced with deserters from our side

6 dareful, beard to beard: boldly, face to face

10 The ... been: once

11-3 My fell of hair ... were in't: Then, a scary story would make my hair stand on end

13 supped full with: filled myself full of

14 Direness: terrible, evil things

15 once start me: scare me now

17-8 She should have ... such a word: *two possible meanings:* She should have died at a later time, not when I have no time to mourn OR She had to die sometime

20 this petty pace: our lives

21 To the last ... time: until the end of the world

22-3 all our yesterdays ... death: the past shows this to be so

111

SHAKESPEARE'S WORLD

FALSE PROPHECIES

People took predicting the future seriously in Shakespeare's time. Both Queen Elizabeth I and King James I used astrologers, and took their advice.

In the world of the play, the Witches seem to predict a future for Macbeth that could never happen. Once the first prophecy comes true, he starts to believe them. His belief is so strong that he bases his decisions on his interpretation of their prophecies.

Many Christians at the time believed that the devil could use false (or misleading) prophecies to tempt people into evil. This is why, when Ross confirms the prophecy that Macbeth will become Thane of Cawdor, Banquo says:

What, can the devil speak true? (Act 1 Scene 3, line 110)

then, later, he says:

And oftentimes, to win us to our harm,

The instruments of darkness tell us truths,

Win us with honest trifles, to betray's

In deepest consequence. (Act 1 Scene 3, lines 127–30)

Banquo was worried that the Witches' prophecies were traps designed to make Macbeth (or him) do terrible things. This question would seem obvious to many people in the original audience. By the end of the play it is clear, his belief in the prophecies has led Macbeth to become a murderer and a tyrant.

Director's view

Bill Buckhurst,
Director, spring 2010

The soldiers are described by Malcolm: "Let every soldier hew him down a bough". And then, in the next scene, he says "Your leafy screens throw down". So you've got literal stage directions. You've got the brutality of this play, and it's quite nice to have something fresh and green and positive arriving in the space. And so we decided to try and follow it literally.

We're going for a backpack with rigid branches [coming] from it. The soldiers are also wearing camouflage and khaki and they also have camouflaged faces. They come through the yard, the first person coming through, Malcolm, parts the way with these two sticks pointing forward. The audience part, and there's this sense of real camaraderie. By this stage, I think everyone has had enough of Macbeth, everyone wants Macbeth out of the way, so they're more than willing to let us through.

Director's Note, 5.5

At Dunsinane Macbeth receives more bad news:

✔ Lady Macbeth is dead;

✔ a wood seems to move towards the castle.

✔ He starts to realise the Witches' prophesies do not guarantee he will succeed. What does he decide to do?

Malcolm's army marches on Dunsinane, using tree branches as camouflage, spring 2010.

1 At the Globe in this production the army marched through the people standing in the yard to watch the play. What effect might this have had on the audience?

2 This production was in modern dress. How well does it work in this scene? Explain your answer.

	Life's but a walking shadow, a poor player
	That struts and frets his hour upon the stage, 25
	And then is heard no more. It is a tale
	Told by an idiot, full of sound and fury,
	Signifying nothing. *Enter a Messenger.*
	Thou com'st to use thy tongue: thy story quickly.

Messenger Gracious my lord, 30
I should report that which I say I saw,
But know not how to do't.

Macbeth Well, say sir.

Messenger As I did stand my watch upon the hill,
I looked toward Birnam, and anon methought 35
The wood began to move.

Macbeth   Liar, and slave!

Messenger Let me endure your wrath, if't be not so.
Within this three mile may you see it coming.
I say, a moving grove.

Macbeth   If thou speak'st false,
Upon the next tree shalt thou hang alive, 40
Till famine cling thee. If thy speech be sooth,
I care not if thou dost for me as much. —
I pull in resolution, and begin
To doubt th' equivocation of the fiend
That lies like truth. "Fear not, till Birnam Wood 45
Do come to Dunsinane", and now a wood
Comes toward Dunsinane. — Arm, arm, and out! —
If this which he avouches does appear,
There is nor flying hence, nor tarrying here.
I 'gin to be a-weary of the sun, 50
And wish th' estate o' the world were now undone. —
Ring the alarum bell! — Blow, wind! come, wrack!
At least we'll die with harness on our back. *Exit all.*

ACT 5 SCENE 6

*Enter soldiers: a drummer, and others with flags, Malcolm,
Siward, Macduff, and their Army, with branches.*

Malcolm Now near enough. Your leafy screens throw down,
And show like those you are. — You, worthy uncle,
Shall with my cousin your right-noble son
Lead our first battle. Worthy Macduff and we
Shall take upon's what else remains to do, 5
According to our order.

Siward   Fare you well.
Do we but find the tyrant's power tonight,
Let us be beaten, if we cannot fight.

Macduff Make all our trumpets speak, give them all breath,
Those clamorous harbingers of blood and death. 10

The drum plays the call to arms, during which they exit.

24 **but a walking shadow:** unreal
24 **player:** actor
31–2 **should report … do't:** don't quite know how to tell you what I saw
34 **did stand my watch:** kept guard
35 **anon:** soon after
39 **grove:** small wood
40 **next:** nearest
41 **famine cling thee:** you starve to death
41 **sooth:** the truth
42 **pull in resolution:** rein in my certainty
44–5 **th' equivocation … truth:** the promises of the Witches where truth and lies become confused
48 **avouches:** claims to be true
49 **There is nor … tarrying here:** It will be impossible to escape or to stay here
50 **'gin to be … sun:** am getting tired of life
51 **th' estate … now undone:** the world would fall apart
52 **wrack:** revenge
53 **harness:** armour
2 **show like those you are:** let them see what you really are
4 **first battle:** main part of the army
6 **order:** battle plan
7 **Do we but … power:** If we can find Macbeth's army
10 **clamorous harbingers:** loud messengers

113

Macbeth and Macduff, summer 2010.

/ Elliot Cowan, r Keith Dunphy

FROM THE REHEARSAL ROOM...

WALK OF SHAME

- In pairs, read Macduff's lines in this scene (pages 117 and 119).

- Look for the words or phrases that Macduff uses to describe Macbeth. Select your favourite of these words or phrases.

- Think of a physical action or gesture that fits with your word or phrase.

- As a whole group stand in two straight lines with an aisle of about a metre wide. Make sure everybody is standing opposite somebody else.

- At the same time, everybody should call out their word/phrase with their action. Then keep repeating your word/ phrase with the action.

- Each person takes it in turn to walk down the aisle in character as Macbeth.

- As you walk down the aisle, you listen to the words/phrases and think about how it feels to walk down the 'Walk of Shame'.

- When you have finished walking down the aisle join the end of the line and continue calling out your word/ phrase.

1 How did it feel to walk down the 'Walk of Shame'?

2 How might an actor use these feelings when playing at this point in the play? Explain your answer.

3 How is this different to the 'Walk of Fame'?

4 Chart Macbeth's journey from the 'Walk of Fame' (page 12) to the 'Walk of Shame'.

Drums offstage play the call to arms, the sounds of a battle.
Enter Macbeth.

Macbeth They have tied me to a stake, I cannot fly,
But, bear-like I must fight the course. What's he
That was not born of woman? Such a one
Am I to fear, or none.

Enter Young Siward.

Young Siward What is thy name?   5

Macbeth Thou'lt be afraid to hear it.

Young Siward No, though thou call'st thyself a hotter name
Than any is in hell.

Macbeth   My name's Macbeth.

Young Siward The devil himself could not pronounce a title
More hateful to mine ear.   10

Macbeth No, nor more fearful.

Young Siward Thou liest, abhorred tyrant, with my sword
I'll prove the lie thou speak'st.

They fight, Young Siward is killed.

Macbeth Thou wast born of woman.
But swords I smile at, weapons laugh to scorn,   15
Brandished by man that's of a woman born. *Exit.*

Drums offstage play the call to arms, the sounds of a battle.
Enter Macduff.

Macduff That way the noise is. Tyrant show thy face!
If thou be'st slain and with no stroke of mine,
My wife and children's ghosts will haunt me still.
I cannot strike at wretched kerns, whose arms 20
Are hired to bear their staves; either thou, Macbeth,
Or else my sword with an unbattered edge
I sheathe again undeeded. There thou shouldst be,
By this great clatter, one of greatest note
Seems bruited. Let me find him Fortune, 25
And more I beg not. *Exit.*

Drums offstage play the call to arms, the sounds of a battle.
Enter Malcolm and Siward.

Siward This way, my lord, the castle's gently rendered.
The tyrant's people on both sides do fight,
The noble thanes do bravely in the war,
The day almost itself professes yours, 30
And little is to do.

Malcolm We have met with foes
That strike beside us.

Siward Enter, sir, the castle.

1–2 **They have tied ... course:** I'm trapped, like a bear being baited (see box opposite).

2–3 **What's he That ... woman?:** What sort of man could possibly not be born from a woman?

12 **abhorred:** hated, loathed

18 **with no stroke of mine:** not by me

20–1 **kerns, whose arms ... staves:** hired foot soldiers

22 **unbattered:** unused

23 **undeeded:** without having used it

24–5 **By this great ... bruited:** someone important must be fighting where all that noise is

27 **gently rendered:** given up, without much resistance

30 **The day almost ... yours:** we have as good as won

32–3 **We have met ... beside us:** Our enemies have changed sides to fight with us

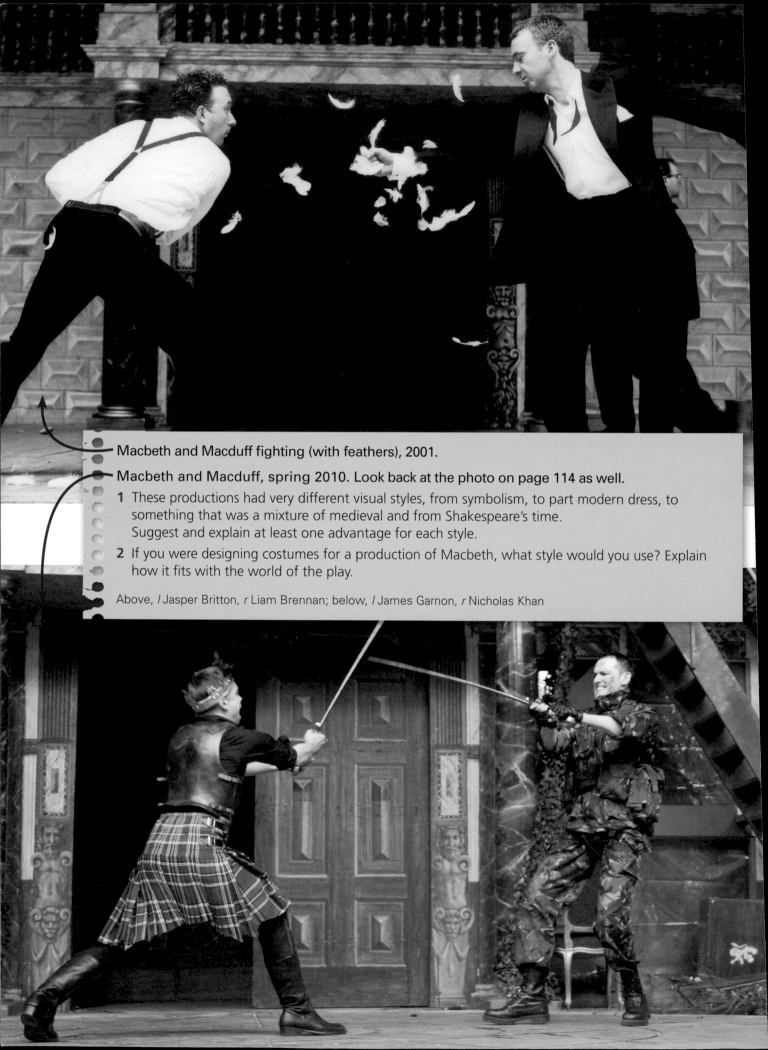

Macbeth and Macduff fighting (with feathers), 2001.

Macbeth and Macduff, spring 2010. Look back at the photo on page 114 as well.

1 These productions had very different visual styles, from symbolism, to part modern dress, to something that was a mixture of medieval and from Shakespeare's time.
Suggest and explain at least one advantage for each style.

2 If you were designing costumes for a production of Macbeth, what style would you use? Explain how it fits with the world of the play.

Above, *l* Jasper Britton, *r* Liam Brennan; below, *l* James Garnon, *r* Nicholas Khan

They exit. Drums offstage play the call to arms, the sounds of a battle. Enter Macbeth.

Macbeth	Why should I play the Roman fool, and die	35
	On mine own sword? Whiles I see lives, the gashes	
	Do better upon them.	

Enter Macduff.

Macduff   Turn hell-hound, turn!

Macbeth   Of all men else I have avoided thee.
But get thee back, my soul is too much charg'd
With blood of thine already.   40

Macduff   I have no words,
My voice is in my sword, thou bloodier villain
Than terms can give thee out.   *They fight. Alarum.*

Macbeth   Thou losest labour.
As easy may'st thou the intrenchant air   45
With thy keen sword impress, as make me bleed.
Let fall thy blade on vulnerable crests,
I bear a charmèd life, which must not yield
To one of woman born.

Macduff   Despair thy charm,
And let the angel whom thou still hast served   50
Tell thee, Macduff was from his mother's womb
Untimely ripped.

Macbeth   Accursèd be that tongue that tells me so,
For it hath cowed my better part of man.
And be these juggling fiends no more believed   55
That palter with us in a double sense,
That keep the word of promise to our ear
And break it to our hope. I'll not fight with thee.

Macduff   Then yield thee, coward,
And live to be the show and gaze o' th' time.   60
We'll have thee, as our rarer monsters are,
Painted upon a pole, and underwrit,
"Here may you see the tyrant."

Macbeth   I will not yield
To kiss the ground before young Malcolm's feet, 65
And to be baited with the rabble's curse.
Though Birnam wood be come to Dunsinane,
And thou opposed, being of no woman born,
Yet I will try the last. Before my body,
I throw my warlike shield. Lay on, Macduff,   70
And damned be him that first cries "Hold, enough!"

They exit, fighting. Drums offstage play the call to arms, the sounds of a battle.
Re-enter Macbeth and Macduff, fighting. Macbeth is killed.
Macduff exits, with Macbeth's body.

35 **the Roman fool:** some Roman generals committed suicide when defeated
36 **lives:** living enemies

38 **Of all men else:** More than any other man
39 **charg'd:** weighed down with
40 **blood of thine:** your family's blood
43 **terms can give thee out:** words can say
44 **losest labour:** are wasting your time
45 **intrenchant:** uncuttable
46 **keen:** sharp
46 **impress:** make a mark on
47 **vulnerable crests:** the heads of men who can be wounded
49 **Despair thy charm:** your magic protection is worthless
50 **angel:** evil guiding spirit
52 **Untimely ripped:** born by Caesarian operation, not born naturally
54 **cowed my … man:** taken away my courage
55-6 **juggling fiends … double sense:** Witches who deceive us by using double meaning
57-8 **keep the word … hope:** make promises that seem true but let us down
60 **show and gaze … time:** a public amusement for many years
62 **Painted upon … underwrit:** with your picture on a sign outside the sideshow tent that says
66 **baited with the rabble's curse:** shown off for the public to curse
68 **thou opposed:** you, my opponent
69 **try the last:** fight to the end
69 **before:** in front of
70 **Lay on:** Let's go
71 **Hold, enough:** Stop, I give in

Director's Note, 5.7

✔ In the battle, Macduff searches for Macbeth.

✔ Macduff tells Macbeth he was not 'of woman born'. They fight, and Macduff kills him.

Drums play the Retreat, then Trumpets a fanfare. Enter Soldiers with drum and flags, then Malcolm, Siward, Ross, Thanes, and Soldiers.

Malcolm I would the friends we miss were safe arrived.

Siward Some must go off: and yet by these I see,
So great a day as this is cheaply bought.

Malcolm Macduff is missing, and your noble son.

Ross Your son, my lord, has paid a soldier's debt,   5
He only lived but till he was a man,
The which no sooner had his prowess confirmed
In the unshrinking station where he fought,
But like a man he died.

Siward   Then is he dead?

Ross Ay, and brought off the field. Your cause of sorrow   10
Must not be measured by his worth, for then
It hath no end.

Siward   Had he his hurts before?

Ross Ay, on the front.

Siward Why then, God's soldier be he.
Had I as many sons as I have hairs,   15
I would not wish them to a fairer death:
And so his knell is knolled.

Malcolm   He's worth more sorrow,
And that I'll spend for him.

Siward   He's worth no more.
They say he parted well, and paid his score,
And so God be with him. — Here comes newer comfort.   20

Enter Macduff, with Macbeth's head.

Macduff Hail, king, for so thou art. Behold, where stands
The usurper's cursed head. The time is free.
I see thee compassed with thy kingdom's pearl,
That speak my salutation in their minds;
Whose voices I desire aloud with mine.   25
Hail, King of Scotland!

All   Hail, King of Scotland!

Fanfare of trumpets.

Malcolm We shall not spend a large expense of time
Before we reckon with your several loves,
And make us even with you. My thanes and kinsmen,
Henceforth be earls, the first that ever Scotland   30
In such an honour named. What's more to do,
Which would be planted newly with the time,
As calling home our exiled friends abroad
That fled the snares of watchful tyranny,

1 **I would:** If only
1 **we miss:** who aren't here
2 **must go off:** must be dead
2–3 **by these I see ... bought:** seeing who is here, you've lost very few to win a great victory
5 **paid a soldier's debt:** died in battle
7–8 **The which ... fought:** and as soon as he had proved he was a man by fighting well and bravely
10–1 **cause of sorrow ... worth:** grief must not be as great as his nobility
16 **I would ... death:** I couldn't hope for a better death for them
17 **And so his knell is knolled:** And that's his epitaph
19 **parted:** died
19 **paid his score:** did his duty (literally, paid his bills)
20 **newer comfort:** more up-to-date and cheering news
22 **The usurper:** the person who stole your throne (Macbeth)
22 **The time:** now we are
23 **compassed:** surrounded by
23 **pearl:** best nobles
24–5 **That speak ... with mine:** who I know agree with me and I ask them to join me in saying
28–9 **reckon with your ... with you:** reward you for your support
30 **Henceforth:** From now on
32 **Which would be ... time:** to make a fresh start
33 **As:** includes
34 **snares:** traps
34 **watchful tyranny:** Macbeth's spies

Director's Note, 5.8

✔ Malcolm won the battle. Macduff brings him Macbeth's head.
✔ Malcolm rewards his followers by making some of them Earls.

Producing forth the cruel ministers   35
Of this dead butcher and his fiend-like queen
(Who, as 'tis thought, by self and violent hands,
Took off her life). This, and what needful else
That calls upon us, by the grace of Grace,
We will perform in measure, time and place.   40
So thanks to all at once and to each one,
Whom we invite to see us crowned at Scone.

A trumpet fanfare.   *Exit all.*

35 Producing forth: finding
35 ministers: servants, officials
37–8 by self and violent ... life: committed suicide
38–9 what needful ... upon us: any other duties I must carry out
39 by grace of Grace: with God's help
40 measure, time and place: carefully, at the right time and in the right place

Macduff displays Macbeth's head. Malcolm, with his back to us.

What did Shakespeare do at the end of the fight (page 117), to set up this moment?

Nicholas Khan, Philip Cumbus

These questions help you to explore many aspects of Macbeth. At GCSE, your teacher will tell you which aspects are relevant to how your Shakespeare response will be assessed.

EXAMINER'S TIP

A good response

A good response may make links between details in a scene and details in a scene before or after. This can show either that Shakespeare is sustaining an aspect of plot or character (i.e. doing something to reinforce it) or developing an aspect of plot character (i.e. making it more varied or complex).

A simple structure of comment can do this: 'Here we see Macbeth being bold and defiant – just as before.' (sustain) or 'Here we see Macbeth feeling hopeless, which is a change from before.' (develop).

1 Character and plot development

Shakespeare creates a fast-moving final Act, with short scenes and rapidly changing settings and characters. He shows Macbeth's sudden swings between fear, rage, determination and hope as he clings onto power. The world around Macbeth is no longer under his control. He goes from villain to tragic victim of his own acts. This is in sharp contrast to the heroism of Act 1.

1   How does Shakespeare continue Macbeth's mixture of impressive determination and savagery in Scene 7, lines 1–37? Pick out lines carefully to prove your point.

2   What makes Macbeth seem, surprisingly, a man who still has a sense of conscience and regret when he faces Macduff in Scene 7? Think about what he does and what he says.

3   Macbeth declares he will not fight Macduff, but Macduff's words make him realise that there are some conditions under which he would not choose to live. What are they?

2 Characterisation and voice: dramatic language

Shakespeare writes speech that brings out the difference between characters, such as the Porter, the Witches, Lady Macbeth and the group of thanes. He also writes speech that brings out the different parts within characters. Macbeth is given different voices for different moods and attitudes, such as confidence and doubt. At this point, he uses voice effects to bring out the conflict in Macbeth between brave defiance and authority, and feelings of insecurity.

4   Which word in Scene 7, line 35 cues an actor to show contempt for the Roman tradition of committing suicide rather than live as a conquered man?

5   Which word in lines 38–40, even at this late stage, suggests that Macbeth still has a conscience?

6   How does Macduff's speech after his entrance remind us of Macbeth's links with the forces of the devil?

7   What attitude do you think Macbeth is showing at line 44: 'Thou losest labour'?

3 Themes and ideas

Last acts often wrap up the action with some sense of meaning or purpose.

8   How do the refrences to God in Scene 8 link with a return to God's order on earth?

9   What suggests a return to a more just social order? Look at what Malcolm says.

10 What does Siward's response to his son's death bring to the end of the play? How might an audience react to this attitude? Consider the possible reactions of an audience in Shakespeare's time and today.

4 **Performance**

The pace and variety of action in Act 5 provides many opportunities for staging in a theatre. Armies advance disguised as trees, hand-to-hand fights take place with Macbeth, and Malcolm is proclaimed king.

11 According to the stage directions at the end of Scene 7, what would you want to be happening on stage, and for how long, to make this a dramatic end to the scene?

12 How would you make the most of the stage directions at the beginning of Scene 8?

13 What advice would you give to the actors playing Siward, Ross and Macduff at line 26 to make the most effective display of ceremony at this closing point of the play?

5 **Contexts and responses**

At the end of the play an audience may feel it has watched a moral fable, a history lesson or a big action entertainment. Which of the following responses is closest to yours – and which do you think likely in Shakespeare's day? Give reasons for your opinions.

14 **a)** Good riddance to the dead butcher!
   b) What a shame: if he'd been willing to settle for less, he'd have had more than most people dream of.

15 **a)** Kings are God's representatives on Earth, so Macbeth's offence was against God as well as Duncan.
   b) Duncan had the Thane of Cawdor killed then he got killed and then Macbeth got killed – it's dog eat dog when Power is at stake.

16 **a)** It's the Garden of Eden all over again – like Adam losing Paradise because his wife was tempted and got him into trouble.
   b) Three foul hags and a fiend-like wife – he never stood a chance against women like these.

17 **a)** He had free choice all the way but chose the wrong path every time.
   b) He never stood a chance because the Dark Forces had chosen him as their victim and plaything.

6 **Reflecting on the play**

18 'We hear the conflict between parts of Macbeth's complex character in his voice and in his language.' How has Shakespeare created such conflict and such a complex character on stage?

19 Throughout the play we are reminded that Macbeth has choices – to follow his conscience or to go against religion, society and nature. Are the choices always presented as a choice between good and evil?

20 Choose a soliloquy you think is most important in the play. Explain why it is important and how it might be performed on stage for maximum impact on the audience.

EXAMINER'S TIP

Writing about drama
Dramatic writing has to keep an audience engaged. Chart the different moods, characters and settings covered in any one of the five acts to see how Shakespeare keeps his audience curious, involved and sometimes, even in a play like Macbeth, caught between laughter and horror.

Reflecting on the play
When writing about a character in a play, even an evil man like Macbeth, remember to comment on how he or she may show motives, feelings and reactions that are typical of ordinary people, or even ourselves. This helps to show appreciation of Shakespeare's skill in showing common human elements in characters on stage – and making us sometimes empathise with them as well as judge them.

1.1	A storm. Three Witches plan to meet Macbeth.
1.2	King Duncan hears that his army has defeated the rebels. He has the Thane of Cawdor, who betrayed him, executed and will give his title to Macbeth.
1.3	The Witches tell Macbeth he will become Thane of Cawdor and then king. They tell Banquo his sons will be kings. Ross arrives and informs Macbeth he is Thane of Cawdor. Macbeth starts to think about becoming king.
1.4	Duncan praises Macbeth and Banquo, names Malcolm as the next king, and plans to visit Macbeth in his castle.
1.5	Lady Macbeth reads a letter from Macbeth telling her about the Witches. When he arrives, she persuades him to murder Duncan.
1.6	Lady Macbeth welcomes Duncan and his court.
1.7	Macbeth decides not to murder Duncan; Lady Macbeth changes his mind.
2.1	Macbeth meets Banquo and his son, Fleance. After they go, he is troubled, and thinks he sees a dagger leading him to Duncan's room.
2.2	Macbeth has killed Duncan but does not leave the daggers. Lady Macbeth takes them back to implicate the grooms. Somebody knocks at the gate.
2.3	The Porter lets in Macduff and Lennox. Macduff discovers Duncan is dead. Macbeth kills the grooms. Duncan's sons flee.
2.4	Macduff reports the belief that the grooms killed Duncan, that Duncan's sons have fled, and that Macbeth has been chosen king.
3.1	Banquo suspects Macbeth. Macbeth plans to murder Banquo and Fleance.
3.2	Macbeth does not tell Lady Macbeth his plan to have Banquo murdered.
3.3	The murderers kill Banquo, but Fleance escapes.
3.4	At a banquet, Macbeth (and only Macbeth) sees Banquo's ghost. His reaction unsettles his guests. He decides to re-visit the Witches.
3.5	Hecate tells the Witches their prophecies will destroy Macbeth.
3.6	Lennox and a Lord discuss their suspicions of Macbeth, and report that Macduff has gone to England to join Malcolm, who is raising an army.
4.1	The Witches show Macbeth apparitions, whose promises convince him he is safe unless Birnam Wood comes to Dunsinane and he can't be harmed by one 'of woman born'. He orders the killing of Macduff's family.
4.2	Macbeth's men murder Lady Macduff and her children.
4.3	Macduff joins Malcolm in England. Ross arrives with news of the murder of Macduff's family. They agree to invade Scotland with the help of England.
5.1	Lady Macbeth is observed by a Doctor and a Gentlewoman walking in her sleep.
5.2	Malcolm's army invades, and Scottish rebels join him.
5.3	Macbeth's supporters are deserting. The doctor cannot cure Lady Macbeth.
5.4	Malcolm orders his solders to cut branches from Birnam Wood to use as camouflage as they move to attack Macbeth in Dunsinane Castle.
5.5	Macbeth is told of his wife's death, and that a wood seems to be advancing on the castle. He starts to doubt the Witches' prophecies.
5.6	Malcolm's army attacks.
5.7	Macbeth kills Young Siward, but is killed by Macduff.
5.8	Malcolm is proclaimed king.

How to write a good response to Macbeth for GCSE English Literature

Whatever Controlled Assessment task or examination questions you take will be based on some of the Assessment Objectives below. Your teacher will tell you which ones are relevant to how your Shakespeare response will be assessed.

If you are taking GCSE English or GCSE English Language, some of the examples for the GCSE English Literature Assessment Objectives may be of use when preparing for your response to *Macbeth*. Your teacher will tell you which ones are relevant to how your Shakespeare response will be assessed.

GCSE English Literature Assessment Objectives

AO	Assessment Objective	Key word used for each AO, below
1	Respond to texts critically and imaginatively; select and evaluate relevant textual detail to illustrate and support interpretations.	**Response**
2	Explain how language, structure and form contribute to writers' presentation of ideas, themes and settings.	**Language**
3	Make comparisons and explain links between texts, evaluating writers' different ways of expressing meaning and achieving effects.	**Comparison/Links**
4	Relate texts to their social, cultural and historical contexts; explain how texts have been influential and significant to self and other readers in different contexts.	**Contexts**

Response

If you are assessed on Response (AO1), you need to:

- understand what you have read and can prove that you understand
- show some judgement based on informed knowledge about plays, language and Shakespeare but also based on your own feelings, attitudes and preferences
- always support what you write with relevant reference or quotation.

How do you show you can do this?

Write a comment on what Macbeth says, showing not just that you understand what he means, but how you can justify your comment by further comment on a detail of quotation. Look at the two examples below, about Act 3 Scene 4:

Rather than: *By this time he knows he can't change anything so he has to carry on killing more and more people.*

Write something such as: *By this time he knows he can't change anything so he has to carry on killing more and more people. When he says, 'I am in blood stepped in so far, that returning should I wade no more were as tedious as to go o'er' it shows that he has thought about 'returning' but knows that this would be just as hard as carrying on, or 'go o'er', it's as if he feels trapped and has no real choice because of what he has already done, and can't change his ways even if he wanted to.*

① Now try it yourself with the question:

What are Macbeth's feelings in Act 2 Scene 1 lines 41–57?

Rather than: *Macbeth's mind is very disturbed at this point because he thinks he can see a bloody dagger in front of him,* using one or two quotations, write a short paragraph in response showing that he partly believes it but also thinks that it may be an illusion.

EXAMINER'S TIP

Response

- Respond thoughtfully and sensitively to the text.
- Pick out short, relevant phrases or quotations from the play to back up your ideas.
- Explain and analyse the quotations.

EXAMINER'S TIP

Language

- Write about why Shakespeare has chosen particular words or phrases to get his meaning across.
- Write about the theme(s) of the play.
- Write about the setting of the play/particular scene.

Language

If you are assessed on Language (AO2), you need to have a good understanding of the writer's craft, including Shakespeare's technical skill in:

- choice of language
- composition of a text in scenes
- making people and situations believable
- making themes and ideas interesting.

How do you show you can do this?

Write a comment which shows that Shakespeare has used particular words and images in a speech so as to have an impact on the audience. Look at the two examples below, about Act 1 Scene 7:

Rather than: *Lady Macbeth shows how she would put her feelings aside by saying she would murder her own child if she had to.*

Write something such as: *Shakespeare shows Lady Macbeth's willingness to kill her own child if she had to, using violent words such as 'plucked' her nipple from his mouth and 'dashed' the brains out. Shakespeare shows how she would have no feelings even though the baby was 'smiling in my face'. This makes her statement seem graphic and physical, and makes her seem equal in brutality to her husband, who can be just as brutal in battle.*

2 Now try it yourself with the question:

Which words has Shakespeare used to suggest strong feelings in Lady Macbeth in Act 1 Scene 5 lines 37–52?

Rather than: *Lady Macbeth shows how evil she is here because she wants evil spirits to help her to do evil,* using one or two quotations, write a short paragraph in response showing that she knows she is doing wrong but still intends to go ahead.

Companion/Links

If you are assessed on Comparison/Links (AO3), you need to:

- see what is similar in texts (e.g. themes. settings, situations) and what is different in texts (e.g. authors' attitudes, values, style and appeal to readers)
- give your opinion of how well the writers have used their craft to create effects on readers/audiences.

How do you show you can do this?

Your comparison or links with *Macbeth* will depend on the linked text you are studying. The example below uses the word 'Text' to reflect this. It shows a comparison/link with a text where a setting can be directly described and *Macbeth* where Shakespeare has to use characters to set the scene, through their dialogue.

If commenting on Act 2 Scene 2, for example, rather than: *In this Text the scene can be set by the author building a description directly into the narrative and setting but in Macbeth Shakespeare has to let the characters set the scene through what they say.*

EXAMINER'S TIP

Comparison/Links

Think about what is similar and what is different about the texts and the way they are written.

Write something such as: *In this Text the writer can build a description of a scene into the narrative and setting by telling the reader, for example: 'The room was dark and the curtains fluttered in the moonlight coming through the half-open window.' In Macbeth, Shakespeare has to create a sense of place and mood by what the characters say, as in: 'Hark! Peace. It was the owl that shrieked, the fatal bellman... The doors are open; and the surfeited grooms do mock their charge with snores...' This is where dialogue fills in the details of what's happening or what's happened offstage.*

3 Now try it yourself with the question:

How does Shakespeare use Banquo's description of Macbeth's castle (Act 1 Scene 6) to create a sense of place? How does this compare with how a sense of place is created in the linked Text you are studying?

Rather than *Banquo describes the castle in a lot of detail so the audience can imagine it, because Shakespeare couldn't put a real castle on stage,* using one or two quotations, write a short paragraph in response, showing how Shakespeare uses the detail in Banquo's speech to convey a sense of time and place. Compare it with an example of how a sense of place is created in your linked Text.

Contexts

If you are assessed on Contexts (AO4), you need to:

- understand something about the culture that is reflected in the text because of the time or place it was written, or how it reflects some aspect of the author's experience
- think about and explain what it is in your own life and culture that makes you interested (or not interested) in the text you have studied
- consider a personal response, but always remember to put your personal feelings in a context of attitudes, values and beliefs that make up your personal culture. The most important thing about social, cultural, or historical contexts is 'What's changed?' and 'What's stayed the same?'

How do you show you can do this?
Rather than: *People in Shakespeare's day would have thought that the Witches were real and had real supernatural power, and were doing the Devil's work.*

Write something such as: *In Shakespeare's day the black and midnight hags would have had a lot of impact on stage because many people believed in the supernatural and thought that night-time was when evil spirits went about. Nowadays, most people don't believe in these things, so the Witches may be seen as Macbeth's imagination at work. In some stage productions, the Witches don't appear on stage, but as voices inside Macbeth's head.*

4 Now try it yourself with the question:

'Doing wrong is doing wrong whenever it happens.' Explain why you agree or disagree with this view that Jacobean and modern audiences would react the same way to Macbeth's plan.

Rather than: *In Shakespeare's day, the Witches would be to blame because they put the idea into his head,* using one or two quotations, write a short paragraph in response, showing that a modern audience may not think that Macbeth was just a passive victim of the Witches.

Key terms

These key terms provide a starting place for exploring key aspects of *Macbeth*. At GCSE, your teacher will tell you which examples are most relevant to how your Shakespeare response will be assessed.

THEMES AND IDEAS

Ambition/power

The Witches rouse Macbeth's ambition to become king 1.3.51; 1.3.148–9; 1.4. 48–52

Macbeth's ambition is balanced by his view of honour 1.7. 12–28

Lady Macbeth's ambition influences Macbeth to kill 1.7

Macbeth and Lady Macbeth's ambition lead to the murder of Duncan 2.2

Macbeth's continuing ambition leads to the abuse of power, the appearance of power and then the loss of power, influenced by the Witches, with the murder of Banquo 3.1. 124–155, Macduff's family 4.1. 154–9; 4.2 and his own death 5.7. 70

Appearance and reality

The hypocrisy and deception of Macbeth and Lady Macbeth

Macbeth makes a loyal speech while already plotting against Duncan 1.4. 22–27 as does Lady Macbeth 1.6. 15–21

Lady Macbeth tells Macbeth to 'Look like th'innocent flower/But be the serpent under't' 1.5. 64–5

Before killing Duncan, Macbeth says they must sustain their false show of honouring the king 1.7. 82–3

Lady Macbeth incriminates the servants by daubing them with Duncan's blood 2.2. 62–67

Both Macbeth's hide their guilt when the body is discovered 2.3

Macbeth tricks Banquo with friendly speech while plotting his murder 3.1. 11–47

When Macbeth sees Banquo's ghost, and talks to it, Lady Macbeth pretends to the guests that this is a recurring illness 3.4

Supernatural appearances

A dagger appears to Macbeth as he struggles with his conscience before killing Duncan 2.1. 41–49

Banquo's ghost appears only to Macbeth after Macbeth had him murdered 3.4

The Witches show Macbeth the eight kings that will descend from Banquo 4.1. 115–128

The appearances and deception of the Witches

The seeming promise of good fortune in future new titles for Macbeth 1.3. 49–51

The prophecies that make it seem impossible that Macbeth will ever be vanquish'd 4.1. 83–98

The deception of the Witches is revealed 5.5. 33; 5.7.48–52

Choices

Macbeth chooses to let the Witches influence his thoughts and actions 1.3.131–150, 1.4. 48–51

Banquo is wary of the Witches and warns against them 1.3. 126–130

Lady Macbeth influences Macbeth's choice to murder Duncan 1.7

Macbeth's choice to murder Duncan 1.7. 80–83 then Banquo 3.1. 124–155 before going back to the Witches 3.4.141–3, 4.1. 47 and choosing to murder the Macduffs 4.1. 155–9

Lady Macbeth suffers the consequence of her choices: sleepwalking and becoming overwhelmed by her guilt 5.1; her death is reported in 5.5. 16: it is thought to be suicide 5.8.36–38

Conflict/Good and evil

Conflicting views of the Witches: Banquo warns against them in 1.3. 126–30 while Macbeth's actions are influenced by their predictions 1.3. 134–146

Conflict within a character; e.g. between good and evil: Macbeth struggles with his conscience before deciding to murder Duncan 1.7. 1–28 and after murdering him 2.2. 27–87

Conflict within the Macbeths' marriage as Lady Macbeth goads him to stick with the plan to murder Duncan 1.7. 35–83

Conflict as Macbeth's evil grows and he arranges Banquo's murder 3.1, Macduff and loyal soldiers turn against him 4.1. 146 and he has the Macduff family killed 4.1. 149–161; 4.2

Equivocation/Ambiguity

The Witches equivocate (say something that appears to mean one thing but can also mean another) when they declare 'Fair is foul, and foul is fair' 1.1. 11; Macbeth's first words echo this equivocation which creates a link with the Witches 1.3. 39

Equivocation is used to mislead; e.g. the Witches seem to promise Macbeth he cannot be harmed by anyone of woman born without letting him know this could mean someone born by a caesarean section, like Macduff 4.1. 83

Equivocation is used to create dramatic irony; e.g. when Macbeth hears of Duncan's death, he says, 'Had I but died an hour before this chance, I had lived a blessed time.' 2.3. 95–6

Ross tells Macduff: 'No, they were well at peace, when I did leave 'em', suggesting all is well before explaining the family is murdered 4.3. 198

Guilt

Macbeth feels guilt; e.g. after murdering Duncan 2.2. 27–87, and with Banquo's ghost 3.4. 55–149

Lady Macbeth's guilt leads to her sleepwalking and trying to wash her hands from the blood of Duncan's murder 5.1. 32–48

Macbeth shows signs of guilt in his final fight with Macduff 5.7.38–41

Hero/tragic hero

Macbeth is presented a hero - honourable, valiant, admired and successful 1.2

Macbeth is shown to become a tragic hero

(because of what he's done or is done to him); e.g. his ambition and desire for power 1.3 leads to his murder of Duncan 2.2 and to order Banquo's murder 3.3

The Witches influence Macbeth's desire for security and power 4.1 which leads to the murder of the Macduffs 4.2

Macbeth's wife suffers because of their guilt 5.1 64–71, 5.5, 5.8.36–38

Macbeth realises he has been deceived 5.7, before he is finally killed 5.7 71–end

Justice/judgement

Macbeth fears human justice and God's justice – which may punish misdeeds in the afterlife 1.7. 1–25

Macbeth's evil deeds are challenged by Banquo's ghost visiting him 3.4 38–149

Lady Macbeth suffers agitated sleepwalking and becomes overwhelmed by her guilt 5.1; her death is reported in 5.5. 16; it is thought to be suicide 5.8. 36–38

Macduff takes retribution when he kills Macbeth for killing his family 5.7

The restoration of the rightful King Malcolm 5.8. 21–42

Kingship

Macbeth says King Duncan is an anointed, righteous, just, meek King and he has no good reason to be disloyal 1.7. 16–20

Lady Macbeth hopes that heaven will not stop their murder of Duncan 1.5. 48–52

Macbeth seizes power, usurping Duncan's named heir Malcolm, who flees to England 2.3.143–149; 2.4.27–35

Macbeth's ambition and expectations of Kingship contrasts with Malcolm who shows signs of true kingship and political skills in his treatment of Macduff 4.1 and restoring order 5.8. 27–42

Male/female

The gender of the Witches is disordered 1.3. 46–48

When considering murdering Duncan, Lady Macbeth rejects her femininity; e.g. 1.5. 36–52; 1.7. 54–9; Lady Macbeth says Macbeth is 'too full o' th' milk of human kindness' to kill Duncan and calls his reluctance unmanly 1.5. 14–28

Macbeth distinguishes between manly valour in killing in battle and unmanly murder 1.7. 46–47; Lady Macbeth argues with this sense of manliness 1.7. 49–51; later likening his seeing visions of Banquo to feminine weaknesses 3.4. 62–73

Macduff says feeling grief for his murdered family is manly, as is revenge 4.3. 245–262

Supernatural

The influence of the supernatural is shown in the Witches' appearances, spells and prophecies: 1.1, 1.3, 3.5, 4.1 and their fulfilment 5.5, 5.7

Macbeth sees supernatural apparitions such as a dagger 2.1.41–72 Banquo's ghost 3.4 and the apparitions and show of kings conjured by the witches 4.1

After Duncan's murder it is dark when

it should be light, and the natural world behaves unnaturally 2.3.52–63; 2.4.1–23

CHARACTERISATION AND VOICE

Characterisation

The skill of making an actor playing a part do it so well that the audience believes he is a real person, with a distinct personality, attitudes, feelings and behaviour. Characterisation can be reported (e.g. of Macbeth 1.2. 33–5) or revealed (e.g. Macbeth 1.3. 134–146).
Voice: *see* Examiner's Tip p32

LANGUAGE

Alliteration

Repetition of the same consonant sounds, especially at the beginning of words; e.g. 'If th' assassination,/Could trammel up the consequence and catch/With his surcease, success' 1.7. 2, or 'Go get some water, And wash this filthy witness from your hand' 2.2. 55–56

Assonance

Repetition of vowel sounds to make a line sound longer or more emotional:
'What thou wouldst highly,/That wouldst thou holily; wouldst not play false,/And yet wouldst wrongly win.' 1.5. 18–20

Blank verse

Verse which is not written with a pattern of lines ending with rhyming words, or with a set pattern of lines to a verse. It is more formal than prose but not as formal as rhyming verse, but it has a regular pattern of stresses to help the actor speak, sometimes by leaving out the syllables of ordinary speech; e.g.
'I will advise you where to plant yourselves,/Acquaint you with the perfect spy o'th' time,/The moment on't, for't must be done tonight' 3.1. 141–3

Imagery

Language chosen to put vivid, usually visual images in the audience's head, particularly if Shakespeare is describing something that can't be shown on stage, for example, the metaphors: 'full of scorpions is my mind' 3.2.39; 'this bank and shoal of time' 1.7.6; or 'vaulting ambition which o'erleaps itself' 1.7.27

Animal imagery

Shakespeare refers to savage animals – serpents, 1.5. 65; 'scorpions' 3.2. 39; 'wolf' 2.1. 61; 'rugged Russian bear', 'armed rhinoceros', Hyrcan tiger' 3.4. 106–7 to suggest violence; and gentle animals to suggest contrasting harmlessness: 'temple-haunting martlets' 1.6. 4; 'the poor cat in the adage' 1.7. 45
Sometimes wild and mild animals are used to contrast opposites: 'Dismayed not this Our captains, Macbeth and Banquo? /Yes, As sparrows, eagles; or the hare the lion.' 1.2. 33–35

Blood imagery

The word occurs many times in the play, usually to convey impressions of violence and destruction e.g. the first description of Macbeth: 1.2. 15–23; and after he murders Duncan 2.2, 2.3 115–149
Blood also becomes a symbol of the Macbeth's guilt, and fear of more death as inevitable 3.4. 145–147, accounting for his reluctance to fight Macduff 5.7. 38–40
A sleepwalking Lady Macbeth tries to wash blood from her hands 5.1. 32–47

Night/Darkness imagery

References to night usually suggest danger, and, often, the concealing of true intentions, as in Lady Macbeth's 'Come thick night,/And pall thee in the dunnest smoke of hell' 1.5. 48–49
After Duncan dies it remains night-like even though it should be day, suggesting disorder 2.5–11. 'Dark night strangles the travelling lamp' 2.4. 8

Pentameters/broken pentameters

These are the two-syllable units of a ten-syllable line; e.g. 2.2.11
'*Alack – I am – afraid – they have – awaked.*'
Sometimes Shakespeare shares the pentameter between two speakers; e.g. 2.2.41
M *Stuck in my throat.*
LM   *These deads must not be thought*
See also Iambic pentameters p36

Prose

The language of everyday speech, without a crafted formal pattern of rhyme or regular rhythm; e.g. Macbeth's letter to his wife 1.5.1–12 Frequently, Shakespeare uses prose for lower-class or less important characters such as the Porter: 2.3.1

Rhyme/rhythm

Shakespeare generally uses rhyme for ritual as with the Witches, who speak in rhyming couplets e.g. lines ending in 'trouble/bubble, snake/bake, frog/dog' 4.1. 10–15
He also uses couplets to show that a scene is coming to an end; e.g. 'drowse/rouse, still/ill' 3.2. 55–58
Shakespeare uses a regular beat or stress of syllables in a line to create a rhythm for a ritual effect as with the Witches. He also uses rhythm to help an actor remember lines and deliver them with controlled breathing so all can hear the lines throughout the theatre; e.g. 3.2. 39
'O, **full** of **scorp**ians **is** my **mind**, dear **wife**'!

PERFORMANCE: STAGECRAFT AND THEATRICALITY

Stage directions

Shakespeare writes very few stage directions for an individual actor. Most are suggestions of extras to create a scene, e.g. lords, attendants 3.4; a list of who comes on stage or goes off, e.g. the ghost's appearances and disappearances in 3.4 However, Shakespeare does embed directions in his texts as cues to actors – where to pause, change tone or attention to purpose, e.g. Banquo giving his sword to Fleance 2.1.5 (se Shakespeare's World on p34). *See also* Asides p16

Structure

The way a play is built with different parts doing different jobs, such as setting the scene, introducing a character, developing the character or the plot.
For example:
1.1. Witches, thunder and lightning: introduces supernatural and evil
1.2 Noises of battle off stage – introduces King Duncan and background of the rebellion and Norwegian wars
1.3 More thunder and the Witches again. First appearance of Macbeth, prophecies
1.4 Regal fanfare of trumpets. Duncan rewards Macbeth and makes Malcolm his heir.
1.5 First appearance of Lady Macbeth who hears the news and plans to murder Duncan
Hence all the elements of the play to come have been introduced, with essential features of character and relationships established and the audience kept interested.

Actor's/Director's view

Bill Buckhurst, Director, pp 42, 44, 112
Lady Macbeth (Claire Cox), pp 40, 48, 102; (Laura Rogers), pp 48, 60
Macbeth (James Garnon) pp 68, 110
Malcolm (Philip Cumbus) p 92
Ross (Julius D'Silva) p 68
Witches: First Witch (Janet Fullerlove) p80; Third Witch (Rachel Winters) pp 10, 80

CONTEXTS

Contexts within the play that create a scene or mood

For example, the play begins with thunder and lighting, creating an atmosphere to herald the witches' entrance. This then contrasts with the bustle of battle in the following scene. Shakespeare continues to contrast contexts e.g. England 4.3 vs Scotland; Lady Macbeth in her castle 1.5 vs Lady Macduff in hers 4.2

Context around the play

For example, the way that ideas, customs and events of the Jacobean period, around 1606, are reflected in the play.
See also Shakespeare's World:
Authorship of 3.5 p74
Bear baiting p114
False prophecies p112
Lady Macbeth's position in society p24
Marriage p22
Stage traps p78
Succession p20
Waiting Gentlewoman p100
Weather portents p44
Witches p10

Globe Education Shakespeare
Series Editors: Fiona Banks, Paul Shuter, Patrick Spottiswoode

Steering Committee: Fiona Banks, Ryan Nelson, Paul Shuter, Patrick Spottiswoode, Shirley Wakley

Macbeth

Editors: Fiona Banks, Paul Shuter

Consultant: Shirley Wakley

Play text: Ryan Nelson, Paul Shuter, Patrick Spottiswoode

Glossary: Jane Shuter

Assessment: Senior moderators and senior examiners including Peter Thomas, Paula Adair, Tony Farrell; key terms index: Clare Constant

From the rehearsal room: Fiona Banks, Adam Coleman, Sarah Nunn, Christopher Stafford, Yolanda Vazquez

Shakespeare's World: Farah Karim-Cooper, Sarah Dustagheer, Gwilym Jones, Amy Kenny, Paul Shuter

Dynamic Learning: Ryan Nelson

Progression: Georghia Ellinas, Michael Jones

Globe Education would like to thank our dedicated team of Globe Education Practitioners – who daily bring rehearsal room practices into the classroom for young people at Shakespeare's Globe and around the world. Their work is the inspiration for this series.

Playing Shakespeare with Deutsche Bank
The spring 2010 production of Macbeth, which features in this book, was the 2010 *Playing Shakespeare with Deutsche Bank* production. This is Globe Education's flagship project for London schools, with 16,000 free tickets given to students for a full-scale Shakespeare production created specifically for young people.

The Publishers would like to thank the following for permission to reproduce copyright material:

Photo credits
All photographs are from the Shakespeare's Globe photo library. Donald Cooper, 2001 production; 16, 30, 38, 44, 56, 58, 62, 68, 100, 116. Manuel Harlan, spring 2010 production; 6, 8, 14, 18, 22, 24, 42, 48, 52, 54, 62, 64, 70, 76, 78, 80, 88, 90, 96, 102, 112, 116, 119. Ellie Kurtz, summer 2010 production; 8, 10, 12, 20, 22, 26, 28, 31, 34, 36, 40, 42, 46, 54, 56, 60, 64, 70, 82, 84, 90, 94, 98, 100, 104, 106, 108, 110, 114. Pete Le May, 3 (lower), John Tramper, 3 (top).

Every effort has been made to trace all copyright holders, but if any have been inadvertently overlooked the Publishers will be pleased to make the necessary arrangements at the first opportunity.

Orders: please contact Bookpoint Ltd, 130 Milton Park, Abingdon, Oxon OX14 4SB. Telephone: (44) 01235 827720. Fax: (44) 01235 400454. Lines are open 9.00 – 5.00, Monday to Saturday, with a 24-hour message answering service. Visit our website at www.hoddereducation.co.uk

© The Shakespeare Globe Trust, 2011
First published in 2011 by
Hodder Education,
An Hachette UK Company
338 Euston Road
London NW1 3BH

Impression number   5 4 3
Year   2016 2015 2014   2013 2012

Cover photo Elliott Cowan as Macbeth, summer 2010, photo Ellie Kurtz
Typeset in Garth Graphic Regular 10pt by DC Graphic Design Limited, Swanley Village, Kent
Printed in Dubai

A catalogue record for this title is available from the British Library

ISBN: 978 1444 13662 3